THE GOLDEN BEAN

A Thorpe Branach
Stone Harbor Mystery

by

MICHAEL JOHN DONOHUE

This book is fiction. All the names, characters, organizations and events portrayed in this book are either the product of the author's imagination or are used fictitiously for versimilitude. Any resemblence to any organization or to any person, living or dead, is unintended.

Cover art and design by David Sybert

ISBN 1-57502-236-2

Printed in the USA by

MORRIS PUBLISHING
3212 E. Hwy 30
Kearney, NE 68847
800-650-7888

Dedicated to beach reading.

Also by Michael John Donohue

HARBOR TALES
Stories from Stone Harbor

A NOTE FROM THE AUTHOR

Dear Reader:

THE GOLDEN BEAN first appeared in the Summer of '95 in The Java Journal, as a serial piece which was never completed. By popular demand the rest of the story has been written. It is total fiction. None of the characters are actual people. I reiterate these facts here, because this book falls into the genre of "crime fiction." Naturally, there is a certain degree of violence and suspense in such a story. But Stone Harbor, New Jersey, where much of this story is based, is, thank God, peaceful and non-violent.

Stone Harbor is a small slice of beach upon which many of us spend all or part of the year. Here we find relaxation, friendship, laughter and love. We are safe from the excesses of urban life. We are secure and protected from the lurking dangers we hear about each night on the evening news.

The Stone Harbor of THE GOLDEN BEAN is a fictional island where far-fetched and mysterious schemes unfold. The businesses referred to in this book have never been associated with any criminal activity. I have merely used a familiar setting in which to create a story that hopefully you will find at least mildly entertaining.

Stone Harbor, NJ - May 1996

MICHAEL JOHN DONOHUE

A good stiff slap in the face from a woman is preferable to a letter ten years later. Yet that's exactly what I got. She was 40 and I was 20. I was the small-town boy trying to impress his friends, and she was the lonely divorcee trying to remember what it was like to be young and in love. Now, I was on a flight from New Orleans to Stone Harbor, New Jersey. I had left after that summer. Although no charges were pressed after I killed Liza's husband, I thought it best to get as far away from Stone Harbor as I could.

I was about to touch down in Philly and all because she had pleaded with me through the mail. The letter came the day after the employee party at the Bon Temp Roule, where I had worked as a bartender for the past five years. My studies at Tulane had flagged since I started playing sax. I spent most of my time on the street corners in the French Quarter. I played well enough to fill my sax case with a bunch of change and a few ones and fives mixed in.

She actually had a car meet me at the airport. The cold April winds were howling through the breezeway at Philadelphia International as I stood and looked around for a driver holding my name on a piece of crumpled cardboard. Finally I found it.

He was a balding man, middle-aged Italian with his five-foot-four inch, one hundred ninety-pound body stuffed into a three-piece wool suit. An unlit cigar hung from the corner of his thick-lipped mouth as he twisted from side to side holding the cardboard high over head. Printed on it in black magic marker were two words,

Thorpe Branach.

"I'm Branach," I said to the driver. He lowered his arms and adjusted his cigar. Tilting his head to one side, he looked me over and must have believed me because he grabbed my bag and turned, walking with a slight wobble, toward a big Lincoln Town Car that was idling in the no-standing zone. He tossed the bag in the trunk and opened the rear, left passenger door of the car.

"Thanks," I said loudly. He said nothing. We rode in silence over the Walt Whitman bridge and down the Atlantic City Expressway. Finally we headed south on the Garden State Parkway and made a left at the second light.

Stone Harbor Boulevard had changed a great deal in ten years. There were massive car dealerships where once there were woods and lakes. We wound our way down the Boulevard, passing the now shut-down Topeka Lodge and the crumbling lumber yard. I was amazed as we drove down 96th Street, that Hahn's was gone. So was Hankin's and Laughlin's and a half-dozen other places that I remembered from childhood. All replaced with new, more modern storefronts. We crossed Third Avenue and at Second Avenue I spoke up.

"Make a U-turn, will ya pal?" I said to the smug, little man. He shrugged and sighed and it seemed a gargantuan effort for him to turn the car around. We headed back up 96th Street and I had him pull-up in front of Fred's. I took a deep breath as I stepped from the car and toward the door of Fred's Tavern. It was here that I had met Liza a decade ago. It wasn't too far from here that a lunatic that she had once called husband nearly ended the lives of both of us.

The Tavern was cave-like and smoky, just as I remembered it. I looked around the bar and saw one or two familiar faces. Familiar, but ten years older. Not just ten years, but ten years of sitting at the bar aging quickly.

"What can I getcha?" the bartender asked. I needed the double bourbon. It had been a long time since I had been in Stone Harbor and an even longer time since I had seen Liza. As I drank the whiskey I considered going back to Philly and heading right back to New Orleans. Jazz Fest was right around the corner and . . . oh hell, who was I kidding. I never could say no to her.

Mr. Personality and I headed back down 96th Street. We made a right on First Avenue and headed south. When we got to Nun's Beach the driver looked confused.

"First Avenue ends here. You have to take Second to 132nd Street," I instructed. He turned up the radio and I was forced to listen to the last two minutes of Barry Manilow's "Mandy" as he delivered me to Liza's monstrous house on the beach. The wind off the Atlantic was cold and harsh as I walked up the wide brick driveway. Liza's house was a two-story upside-down house with thc best view of the ocean on the island. The second-floor living room was windows on two sides and emptied out onto a deck bigger than most back yards.

I tried to gather a little courage from the bourbon as I pushed the little illuminated door-bell button. It seemed as though she was standing there waiting for me. The door opened barely a second after I rang the bell and there she was. That tumultuous summer she was a young forty but now, she was a bit weathered at fifty. A life of intense ultraviolet rays on beaches from Stone Harbor to Sydney had made her look so vibrant as a young woman but had cost her her complexion as an older lady. Yet, behind the aging exterior she was there. I could see the pretty young smile I had known. I saw the tracks of her tears, a decade old, but still there. Her body was only twenty when she was forty, now it was about thirty-five. Most of all, I saw the eyes. The same pale, green eyes that had gotten me into so much trouble.

"Hi Thorpe." The voice rattled me and stirred up some long-lost emotion. I tried to respond but my words clung to the inside of my throat and I did little more than choke.

"You O.K.? You look like you've seen a ghost." I had.

"I . . . I'm fine. Sorry, hello." We embraced briefly and the tension began to ease. She led me upstairs and gave me a bourbon.

"Have a seat and catch your breath." Her voice was serious and business-like. I had a feeling she was about to become a customer and not just an old lover.

"Despite the fact that we haven't spoken in years Branach, I have kept track of you. You tried college but that didn't work. You tried music and that didn't work. But somewhere along the way, you developed a knack for, what shall we call it? Recovery work. I found out about the stolen yacht you got back from those nasty people in Jamaica. I also heard about the fifteen carat, uncut South African diamond you smuggled back to its owner out of Germany. You've gotten around."

I smiled and sipped my bourbon.

"I work some, and spend the rest of my time enjoying myself," I said smugly. She didn't smile.

"Look Thorpe, I know that if I found out about these things, there must be others that you didn't brag quite as much about. I don't know how you got into this line of work, but the fact is, I need your services." I wanted to say something crass and sexist but I resisted.

"Liza, I worked for an international courier service and met a lot of people all over the world. A couple times I managed to get things in and out of a few places for some people who have a little operation called Central Intelligence down in Langley, Virginia. It all snowballed from there. I feel like there is so much to be said, but I just don't know. Where do we start?"

"We don't. I didn't ask you to come here for a reunion, Branach. I need you to get something for me."

She handed me a picture of a girl in her mid-twenties, dressed in a sky-blue sundress.

"She's a beauty. Where'd you lose her?"

"Not the girl. That's my daughter." I looked closer and realized it was her daughter. But she was fifteen when I last saw her. She had grown into her mother. It was as though looking at that picture transported me back along the years to that night in Fred's when a lonely and frightened woman told me she needed someone to walk home with because she was afraid of the guy who was trying to pick her up. The young woman in the picture was smiling Liza's smile, but she had the dark, almost black eyes of her father, God rest his murderous soul.

THE GOLDEN BEAN

"It's the necklace I'm looking for." Around the neck of the daughter was a braided gold chain with one large, tear-drop shaped hunk of gold hanging between the collar bones.

"What's so special about a gold necklace that you have to drag me up here and treat me like the help?" She cringed a bit at that and I felt a sense of accomplishment at finally getting her to register some emotion.

"Its not just a necklace. It is the Golden Bean." She must have noticed my puzzled look because she began to explain immediately.

"I'll give you the brief history. In 984 an Ethiopian Prince of the Galla tribe accepted an enormous coffee bean in exchange for letting a brigade of soldiers of some army or another pass through his lands in their attempts to outflank some Turks. The Prince, believing the bean to have unusual powers because of its tremendous size, immediately had it covered in gold and placed on a pillow on an altar. Well, the Turks beat the attack and tortured the truth about the Ethiopian Prince out of the soldiers who had threatened them. The Prince gave the Golden Bean to a Turkish Commander in exchange for his life. The bean changed hands over the centuries until it finally ended up in the possession of Khair Beg in 1511."

"I *beg* your pardon." I mocked.

"Not funny Branach. Khair Beg was the governor of Mecca. He was corrupt and feared the people. He also feared coffee. He saw it as a threat to him. People would meet for coffee and talk politics. Beg outlawed coffee and placed the Golden Bean on a necklace proclaiming that only he could possess coffee and then only the Golden Bean. In 1600 the Golden Bean was given to Pope Clement VIII as spoils of the crusades, and in the late 1930's the Vatican gave the necklace to Mussolini as part of the deal to get Mussolini to leave the Church alone. Well, Il Ducé gave it to his wife. When the Italians finally lynched Mussolini, the Golden Bean disappeared." She took a deep breath and started again. "It resurfaced in the '70's in the possession of Filbert Grey, a British entrepreneur who, coincidentally, was my second husband."

"So that's why you never called." I couldn't help myself. Here was the woman who had defined my life, and she had yet to acknowledge what we had been through.

"Listen, Thorpe, we can get into that at some later date. Right now, the Golden Bean is missing and I want it back."

"What's the matter Liza? Didn't Gilbert Grape leave you a big enough nest egg?"

"Its Filbert Grey, and that has nothing to do with it. That necklace belongs to me and I want it back."

Finally, she sat close beside me and stared at me with those powerful, vampiresse eyes.

"Will you find it for me, Thorpe?" I squirmed a bit and she must have sensed that I was about to say no. I didn't need this. Beckoned from my comfortable life by this shadow of my past. I was going back to New Orleans. The crawdad were big and spicy and Spring was approaching. All I had to do was say no and finally leave this woman behind me. Way behind me.

THE GOLDEN BEAN

"It's worth thirty-seven million dollars," she said.

I said yes.

It had taken her all of ten minutes to convince me that I should spend the Spring and Summer and maybe the entire year chasing after some dusty old coffee bean. Never mind the fact that this coffee bean was over a thousand years old and worth thirty-seven million dollars, I wanted more. I wanted this woman to recognize the fact that what we had been through was not merely some small memory. We had nearly died together.

-2-

It was late June. Stone Harbor was hot, but its not so much the heat as the stupidity. At 20 I was pretty stupid. I'd drink enough liquor in a week to outfit a wedding reception with three open bars. Of course, I tried not to drink on duty. I was a Summer Cop. Rent-a-Cop to most other locals. But I liked the job. They trained me how to defend myself, with my fists and a gun. I walked up and down 96th Street, breaking up fights and scaring away shoplifters.

I had seen Liza one day standing in front of Hoy's 5 & 10. She was pretty. About five-three with dark hair and a San Tropé tan. She asked me for a quarter for the parking meter.

"Sorry ma'am, the police don't carry change." She pierced me with those pale green eyes and, as if through some psychokenesis, I reached into my pocket and pulled out a quarter.

"Thank you so much," she said and trotted over to feed the meter. I was dumbstruck. Somehow she had taken control of me for a moment. I shook it off and continued walking my beat. The worst part of the job was being a local. I had grown up in Stone Harbor. My mother was a teacher at Stone Harbor elementary and my father worked for the Electric Company. Now, as a Summer Cop, I was faced with knowing too much about the illegal business dealings of some of my friends. I had to make decisions about who to arrest when a local and a tourist, or "shoobie," as we call them, got into a fight. It was usually the shoobie.

During one of my many nights spending my paycheck in Fred's, I was confronted once again by the parking meter lady. She caught me coming out of the men's room in the Tavern, as if she had been waiting for me.

"Got a quarter?" she asked. I didn't make the connection until I looked into those eyes.

"Sorry ma'am, the police don't carry quarters," I said, mocking my uniformed tone. We laughed and took care of all the preliminaries, what's your name, where ya from, what do you do? Then she turned serious.

"Thorpe, do you see that man over there?" she asked. I looked over toward the jukebox and saw a man in dark grey shorts and a black, silk, button-down shirt. His gaze kept jumping from the jukebox to Liza and back again. He was about as tall as me, maybe six-four. But he was skinny. His face was pale and his nose ran down the center of it like some squiggly afterthought.

"Yeah, I see him," I told her.

"He's been hitting on me all night. I can't get rid of him." My peacock feathers went up.

"How aggressive was he?" I asked as I felt the adrenalin begin to flow.

"No, no. He wasn't like that." She put her hand on my shoulder and I immediately calmed down. "He just won't stop following me around. Can you just walk me home? I'd feel a lot safer."

I was compelled by my duty as a law enforcement officer to see to this woman in distress. The fact that all of my friends would see me walking out of Fred's with a gorgeous older woman had nothing to do with it.

"Sure," I said. "We can slip out through the liquor store." I pulled open the door that leads from Fred's tavern into the liquor store. The barbacks were locking the liquor store for the night as Liza and I came through the door.

"Hold on a minute there, Johnny," the night manager said to the young man locking the door. "Branach's gotta sneak out the back again." I winked and smiled as I took Liza's hand and we slipped out into Fred's parking lot on 95th Street.

"Where's your house?" I asked.

"I've got a little place down on the bay around 93rd Street." We walked west on 95th Street then took a right on Sunset Drive to get to 93rd.

"Can I ask if you're married?" I said. She shuddered a bit and then told me that she had been married very young. She painted the picture of a manipulative and sadistic man, her ex-husband. A line of thunderstorms had rolled over the island while we were in Fred's, and the night had cooled. You miss a lot sitting at a bar. Her voice was warm and flecked with genuine pain as she told mc the story of her horrible marriage. I could read between the lines and see that there had been violence which was too painful to discuss.

"I can't believe I'm telling you all this," she said as we reached her house. " I feel very comfortable with you."

"Good," I said as I stretched and yawned. "Well, I guess this is good-night."

She smiled, stood on her tip-toes and gave me a peck on the

cheek.

"I'm sure you young guys expect to get invited in every time. But I'm old enough to be your mother and I've got a daughter sleeping in there who could take you to her prom." I shook my head from side to side.

"I have no expectations. I'll see you around I'm sure." She tossed me a "Thanks, Thorpe," as I walked back to Fred's to get my bicycle and make the ride back to 83rd Street where I was living with forty close friends for the summer.

This flashback ended when I felt the cold April wind rolling off the Atlantic. Liza had opened the big sliding-glass door which led out onto her second-floor deck. She walked out and the wind whipped her hair and her clothing. I got up from my seat and met her by the deck rail. The Atlantic was black and raging. Lines of frothy foam tumbled in with the waves that were lit by the quarter moon. I noticed Liza was crying.

"I'm sorry," I said. "Was it something I did?" She wiped her eyes and snuffled.

"No, Thorpe. Its just, seeing you again brings back all those awful memories." It was clear that somewhere in her mind she had traveled back to that night when our worlds had collided and nearly crumbled. I had been trying to avoid it.

"Liza, listen. Let's just, like you said, talk about those things at some other time. Tell me about the Golden Bean. Where is it?" She welcomed the change of topic.

"The last time I saw it, it was in the safe downstairs in this house." She told me but I didn't quite believe that this house in my little town once contained a piece of history worth thirty-seven million dollars.

"You had it here?" I asked with disbelief.

"Yes. Come on, Thorpe, Stone Harbor is not exactly the crime capital of the world. Bikes and skateboards, they get stolen, but you don't hear about Brinks jobs in this town." She had a point. This little slice of beach was the most crime free spot I knew.

She continued as we walked in from the deck, "I left for Europe, my daughter was here. The one in the picture." I looked again at the snapshot she had handed me. The Golden Bean was some hunk of gold. Hung around the daughter's neck, it looked like a golden tear from one of those gargantuan Buddhas you might see in the Far East.

"You remember Deliah, don't you Thorpe?" Liza asked, taking the picture from me.

"Sure. She's grown into a beautiful young lady." Liza studied the picture then tossed it onto the coffee table. "Deliah has her father's eyes. Did you notice?" Liza was too deep into her remembrance of those events to let go. I grabbed her around the shoulders.

"Dammit Liza. I just don't want to go back there. At least not right now. Tell me where this necklace is so I can go get it and get back to living my life." I startled her sufficiently for her to tell me the rest of the story.

Liza was the only person who knew the combination to the safe. Deliah was in the beach house the entire time Liza was away and never left for more than a few hours at a time. There was no sign the safe had been tampered with. The Golden Bean was simply gone when Liza opened the safe upon returning from Europe to lock up some rare stamps.

"What did the cops find?" I asked. She took a deep breath and exhaled slowly.

"Thorpe, this necklace is technically still the property of the Italian government. If it ever changes hands, it does so very discreetly with a hefty sum paid to a few Italian bureaucrats to prevent any investigation. It's not the type of thing one calls the police about. I wanted to find an excuse and bow out of this assignment, but I could use a big chunk of change. At this point my reserves were low and the sax playing in the French Quarter was a hobby that I really didn't want to turn into a job.

"Liza, how do you expect me to find this thing? I go after things when people know where they are. I don't have the time, or the patience, to try and track down something that has utterly disappeared." I was trying to bow out gracefully. If she had no idea where The Golden Bean was, then I was going back to New Orleans on the first flight from Philly.

I noticed the hint of a smile creep across her lips as she began thumbing through a magazine.

"I'm serious," I said with indignance. "I'm outta here in the morning." I started to walk downstairs where I knew there would be bedrooms in the upside-down house.

"Wait, Thorpe, wait. Look at this." She handed me a copy of The New Yorker open to a page headlined "Private Auctions."

"Read the fourth entry," she said excitedly.

"Exclusive arrangement. 10K to open the door.

New and used. Auction closed. Private engagement. Only most sincere and knowledgeable get in. One offering only. Price will not be low. Cash and carry, no deposits. Contact Mr. Green at Tampa number."

I read it a few times and finally said, "Yeah. So?"

"Come on Thorpe, can't you see it? Remember, this necklace once belonged to Mussolini. They called him Il Ducé. Look, skip the first and last sentence, then take the first letter of the last word of each sentence and what do you get?"

I read the section again to myself. "10K to open the door," D. "New and used," D-U. "Auction closed," D-U-C. "Private engagement," D-U-C-E.

"Ducé's gold!" I exclaimed. "My God, would anybody be stupid enough to actually advertise this in The New Yorker?"

She snatched the magazine out of my hand. "Thorpe, its brilliant. Only someone who knows the history is going to know what the code means. Do you really think the Italian government is scanning The New Yorker every week to see if anyone is advertising the auction of the Golden Bean?" She had a point.

"How did you find it?" I asked.

"I didn't, Deliah did. She reads this thing from cover to cover every week and for some reason this caught her eye. You see, she feels somewhat responsible."

"When can I talk to Deliah?" I asked. The excitement ran out of Liza.

"Thorpe, she won't see you. She understands that you only did what was necessary, but she still sees you as the man who killed her father. That's tough to deal with."

* * *

A blindside in football is when one player runs full speed into another, knowing that the other has no idea that the first is coming. The collision is brutal and sometimes tragic. My best friend on the Middle Township Football team was blindsided in the last game of the season. I was at his house the night before the game. He tacked three copies of letters of intention to accept a scholarship to his dart board. One was for Oklahoma. One for Florida. And the other for Clemson. He stood as far away from the dartboard as he could and closed his eyes. The dart flew a wobbly track into the Florida letter and he took it down and signed it. But the next day he was blindsided and never earned a college credit in his life.

It was now late August and Liza and I had developed a very discreet, yet very active relationship. We had traveled through the summer more than happy to have made each other's acquaintance. We had talked once about her past and then the subject was dropped in favor of more enlivening topics. Weeks had passed and we were troubled only by the fact that the Summer was coming to a close.

The sunset that night was a brilliant display of fire-orange and red. Liza and I stood on the pedestrian walkway of the 96th Street bridge and watched nature's second best light show.

"Cook me dinner?" Liza asked as the last sliver of sun slipped away over the horizon.

"Sure," I said, as we headed down the walkway and

across 96th Street to Sunset Drive. As we walked past 95th Street, Liza spoke again.

"Lets go to Fred's and get a bottle of wine," she said. We turned down 95th Street towards Fred's and she started rummaging through her purse.

"What are you looking for?" I asked.

"I had this great wine at the Windrift last weekend. I wrote the name of it down on a matchbook." She rummaged as we walked. Ahead I saw a vaguely familiar figure emerge from a car on 95th Street. My brain scanned its memory to find a matching image. The figure walked diagonally across the Street and leaned up against a telephone pole with a street light on it. In the light I saw the same long, crooked nose I had seen the night Liza had asked me to walk her home from Fred's so many weeks ago. I thought it funny that we were about to walk right past the poor guy.

"Liza, there's your old friend. The weirdo." She gave a disinterested "Huh?" as she rooted through her purse. Finally she looked up. She stopped so abruptly that I was two steps ahead of her before I could turn to see what was wrong. She had dropped her purse and everything from lipstick to TUMS was lying on the sidewalk.

I began to say "What's wrong?" but was cut off by the voice of the odd, thin man.

"Hi, Liza," he said. His voice sounded more like that of an old woman than of a middle-aged man. I turned to look back in his direction and there he was. He was three feet from me and closing. All in one motion he pulled his hand out of the right pocket of his wind-breaker and produced a .38 caliber, snub-nosed revolver. He didn't flinch. He didn't hesitate. He had a sick, twisted smile on his face. I whirled around to my left. I saw cars flying by me. Then I was looking up at the darkening sky with a burning, dampening sensation in my left arm. I tried to lift myself, but my left arm and shoulder were dead weight and my brain hadn't caught up to compensate for the injury from the gunshot.

The next thing I saw was Liza's face over top of me. I thought for a moment that I had just awakened from a nightmare, but then I saw that she was crying. The head of the thin man poked out from behind Liza. He had her by the hair and had the gun pressed against the back of her head. He smiled his twisted smile and I looked him straight in the eye. His eyes were dark and cold, almost black.

"I been watchin' you, Branach. Thought you could steal my wife away from me huh? Well, its all over now, tough guy."

I tried to get up again, but the pain made me convulse. I could feel the rough concrete of the sidewalk against my right cheek. I opened my eyes and three feet from my nose was a Windrift match book that had fallen open. Written on the inside in Liza's feminine scrawl was "Kendal Jackson Cabernet Reserve."

"You look at her, Branach. I want you to see this." He pulled Liza closer to me. "This is it." He said as his demon eyes grew wide. Somewhere down the street a car locked-up its brakes and squealed to a stop. The maniac dropped his gaze for a split second. It was during that split second that I swung both my legs at him, knee high. I felt his right knee buckle and heard it pop as he let out an old woman's shriek. Liza fell and rolled into the curb. The .38 bounced off the sidewalk, its blue steel glistening in the street light. My momentum had carried me onto my knees and the palm of my right hand. My left arm hung there like so much dead meat. The gun was two feet from me and about a foot from Liza's former Mr. Right. He was strong with the pain-killer of insanity and was about to get to his feet. I lunged for the gun, scooped it up, and aimed for the center of the thin mass that was staggering toward me. I squeezed five times and watched as he crumbled like an imploded building, falling in on himself.

Time had not healed these wounds. For any of us. Now, Liza was closing in on AARP membership and I was living a life of benign indifference broken by occasional life-threatening intrigue. And the daughter of the man I had killed looked on me as a murderer, although I was cleared of any wrongdoing.

Liza and I were immersed in our collective memory of the past when the phone rang in the present. She picked it up on the third ring and said a quiet hello. I could hear sound but couldn't make out the words. I stood on the other side of the big living room gazing out at the cold Atlantic and wondering if there was any possible way of actually finding this Golden Bean. When she finished the phone call, I struggled to keep myself from asking who it was. She told me anyway.

"That was Deliah. She's in New York. I told her you had gotten here safely and that you were going to get the necklace back."

"Just like that, huh?" I said. "Did she send her love and wish me luck?" Tension crawled along my spine.

"No, Thorpe," Liza said. "She wanted to know when you'd be gone so she could come down here."

"Look, Liza, I'll try and get this thing back for you, but I make no promises. I need an open line of credit and my fee is half of recovery. You want a business-like atmosphere, here it is. If I get this Golden Bean back, I get half of the thirty-seven million." I had had it. I'd been dragged a thousand miles by long-forgotten memories and forced to relive some of the darkest and brightest moments of my life and I wanted no more of it.

"I'll be outta here tomorrow. You can call her back and tell her that. You know, maybe she would have preferred that both of us were murdered that day." As usual I took things one step too far. I moved my head just enough to avoid being hit by the tumbler Liza had hurled at me, but the vodka and rocks splashed all over me.

"You son-of-a-bitch Branach. Don't drag all this out. You said this was business, that was pretty personal." I spotted my reflection in the big sliding-glass door and began to laugh.

"Quite a reunion, huh Leez?" I said with a chuckle. The stress drained out of her and we both laughed a bit.

"There is also one other bit of compensation I want," I said. She looked startled.

"Don't be sick," I said. "I want the biggest, rarest piece of prime rib Henny's has to offer."

There are few things on Earth that can bring a man

closer to the Creator. Henny's prime rib is one of them. There is something about a four-inch-thick, sixteen ounce slab of prime, grade "A" beef, slow-roasted and served with a side of its own au jus that justifies for a man his hairy back and pointed incisors. We dressed and drove down to the restaurant. There were very few diners on a weekday at night. I had worked at Henny's as a teenager in the dishroom, slopping peoples' unconsumed food into big rubber trashcans. But this night, I was going to enjoy my prime rib with a little bourbon and coke and dream about finding The Golden Bean.

"Branach? Get the hell outta here. It is you." Across the dining room, clearing one of the eight-tops, stood Jimmy Bouzard, a friend of the family and part-owner of the restaurant.

"Damn, Branach, I thought you'd died." I stood and shook Jimmy's hand and introduced Liza.

"And I remember you too," Jimmy said. He ran his hand over his thinning hair and pondered Liza.

"It must be ten years ago, you two use ta run around. Oh yeah, then that shooting thing." The food arrived just in time. "Eat up, eat up, this one's on me," Jimmy said. "I'll talk to ya after you're done." Jimmy shuffled off into the darkness of Henny's vast dining room and Liza and I ate. Prime rib, stuffed potato and cole slaw. Culinary nirvana. Little did I know that it would be the last meal I ever ate with Liza. The Golden Bean was out there waiting for me to find it. If I had known then the price I'd pay, I might have said no.

The next morning I left Stone Harbor for New

Orleans with nothing but the New Yorker article and a line of credit ten thousand dollars long at Liza's bank. I didn't ask where she got such good credit, I just accepted the amount and set off for a binge in New Orleans. She owed me that much. I took a cab from the airport straight to Le Bon Temp Roule on Magazine Street. I was determined to spend some money on myself and my friends and live the next few hours of my life as wildly as I could.

"Hey Thorpe," John the bartender said as I walked up to the weathered old wooden bar.

"I'd like a Bud and a double Beam, John my friend," I said. As he poured the bourbon a look of remembrance came over his face.

"Oh yeah, Thorpe, some girl called and left her number." He handed me a slip of paper. There was a 212 area code, and when I got through, the choking, feminine voice of Deliah said, "Branach, Mom's dead."

MICHAEL JOHN DONOHUE

-3-

The party was over, but I set out to drink twice as much. I awoke that next morning with the news of Liza's death a distant, foggy memory buried somewhere beneath bourbon and shock. I drifted on the edge of sleep and imagined that I had dreamed the phone call from Deliah. As I slowly emerged into the waking world, I could smell the rain that was covering New Orleans on this chilly April morning. I heard the familiar clatter of the streetcar as it made its way down St. Charles Avenue, past the stately old mansions with their wide porches and well groomed lawns. I imagined the scene on the streetcar. The black workers mixed-in with the back-pack-toting college students and the excited and fidgeting tourists.

As I rolled over, my head felt as though it was filled with some awful thick liquid that caused pain when it shifted in my skull. I lifted my right hand to my forehead, and as I sat up I became aware for the first time of another body in my bed. I squinted through the blood-shot slits that passed as eyes that morning and discovered that I was the host to a young Tulane student named Adrian James. She was sound asleep on her left side on the right side of the bed. Adrian and I had dated a few times over the past several months. One night I discovered her in a Tulane hangout, drunk beyond the point of being safe among the predator frat boys. I walked her to her apartment and watched over her as she slept off her night of drowning her sorrows over a mother and father who had decided that they were going to London for Christmas, without Adrian.

It seems that Adrian returned the favor last night. I was still in my jeans and tee shirt. My shoes were on the floor beside the bed, next to the small plastic trashcan that Adrian had apparently brought in from the bathroom in case all that bourbon found its way back out the way it came in.

"You still alive Branach?" Adrian asked as she rubbed her eyes and adjusted her Tulane sweatshirt which had twisted around her during the night. She was a five-foot-four inch, chestnut blonde with only one flaw. She had broken her nose as a child when she fell out of a tree. She hated it. I told her it gave her character and I gave her the ironic nickname of Rocky.

"Yeah, Rock. I am certain that death will be less painful." I stood on shaky, aching knees and walked to the bathroom. The bourbon came out of me by the gallon. I stepped into the shower and turned it on as cold as I could possibly make it. The fog began to lift. It was good to be getting rid of the hangover, but the elimination of the dusty haze of the liquor brought the reality of Liza's death into sharper focus. I didn't want that. Not yet.

"What are you doing, Thorpe?" Adrian asked as I walked, clad in a pair of flannel boxers, to the cabinet where I kept my liquor. "Why don't you crawl back into bed instead of back into that bottle?" She walked over to me, took the rocks glass out of my hand and placed it on the dining room table. I looked over her shoulder out of the window of my studio apartment and saw another streetcar pass.

"I got a better idea, why don't you buy me breakfast."

She rolled her eyes and shook her head.

"Okay," she said grudgingly. I dressed and we hopped a streetcar to the French Quarter. We walked down Bourbon Street. The smell of stale beer was dampened by the rain, yet it made its presence felt in the pit of my stomach. We turned and walked past the St. Louis Cathedral. The Place de Jean Paul Deux was slick and shiny. A few sidewalk artists were setting up big umbrellas over their easels, hoping that the morning rain wouldn't keep the tourists in their hotel rooms.

Adrian and I sat at a small table under the canopy at the Cafe Du Monde. I ordered six beignets and a cafe au lait. As we waited for the donuts to arrive, Adrian reached over and took my right hand in her left.

"Thorpe," she said. "You live a strange life. You said a lot last night. You probably didn't mean to, but you told me all about this Liza and this expensive necklace. You also told me that you were once very deeply in love with this woman." She let go of my hand and leaned back in the wrought-iron chair, casting a long, sideways glance at me. "You better go and put her to rest. Don't bury her in a bottle of bourbon." I took a deep breath, then chose the appropriate wrong answer.

"Are you charging me by the hour for this Doctor, or is this a freebee?" It wasn't what I wanted to say, but it is what came out.

"Don't expect me to fly into some stereotypical feminine rage because of your brash display of male insecurity, Branach. I care about you now as a friend. I would like to stick around long enough to care about you as a lover. But I can get out now without too much damage. My point is, Thorpe, you've got problems. Most of which I think stem from your experiences with this woman. You try to drown them in Jim Beam, but I promise you, they're much better swimmers than you are."

It was profound psycho-babble from a young girl who wanted to be the next Freud, but it was true. Liza was the face at the bottom of my personal abyss. She was the rat gnawing at that small, hot spot at the base of my brain. The beignets and coffee arrived. We ate in silence as a lonely saxophone wailed its mourning song from across the French Market. I downed four of the puffy, powdered-sugar-dusted hunks of fried dough and ordered a second cafe au lait. Adrian reached across the table with a napkin in her hand and wiped the right side of my face.

"Slob," she said. I stared into her rootbeer-colored eyes and followed the crooked line of her nose down to the full, lipstickless lips. It wasn't the face of a super model. But those faces are usually attached to a lifeless, brainless body. No, this was a woman full of life and, I shuddered to think, probably smarter than I.

"You know something Rocky?" I asked as I looked back into her eyes. "After I get back from Stone Harbor, I plan to let you give me a try." She rolled her eyes at my ego-riddled remark.

"You are a son-of-a-bitch Branach." I smiled, and held out a beignet to Adrian. I took a deep breath. As she reached for it, I blew the breath out at the beignet as if it were a stubborn birthday candle. There was an explosion of powdered sugar that engulfed Adrian and coated her from her chestnut hair to her strong chin. She wore a look of excited amazement and it was that image of her that I carried with me back to New Jersey.

THE GOLDEN BEAN

-4-

It was strange to be heading back down Stone Harbor Boulevard again. I had left this little resort island behind because of Liza and I had been drawn back to it by her. I pulled the little black rental car into the driveway of Liza's beach house. There was one other car which I assumed was Deliah's. I carried my duffel bag up the few stairs that led to the door of the house. The door opened as I approached and there in front of me was a twenty-five-year-old Liza with wild, empty eyes. She was dressed in white silk pajamas that highlighted her dark features.

"Hello, Branach." Deliah said as she stepped back to let me pass through the door. I put my bag down and reached for her to give her a greeting kiss. She leaned away from me and I puckered at the air.

"Okay," I said, and grabbed my bag. "Where are you putting me?" She pointed upstairs and walked off toward the back of the house, her dark hair swaying as she strutted away. As I climbed the stairs up to the kitchen and the living room, I felt a shudder creep its cold way up my back and settle at the base of the skull. I could see Liza, her clothes fluttering in the April wind as she stared out at the cold Atlantic. The same cold Atlantic that had taken her life.

I picked up the upstairs phone and called Trent Roberts, a Stone Harbor cop with whom I had grown up. I found Trent at home.

"Branach, you sure know how to drag a black cloud over this town. First the husband, now the wife." Trent and I were never what you would call friends. A fact which gave him even less right to say what he had.

"Look Trent, I didn't call to give you an opportunity to practice your comedy act, I just want to know what happened to Liza." My tone was serious and low.

"O.K., let me get off the cordless." He switched phones and proceeded to give me more details than I thought he would. Liza had drowned. A neighbor had seen her at noon, several hours after I left for New Orleans. I was not a suspect. It was the term "suspect" that got my full attention. Trent Roberts went on to tell me that there were bruises on Liza's wrists and, although it had rained that night, and the murderer had tried to cover them up, there were two sets of footprints on the beach in front of Liza's house. The body was discovered in the surf at 95th Street by two local surfers who were taking advantage of an early spring swell. Upon searching the house, the police found a ragged hole in a wall were a safe had once been. The medical examiner reported that Liza had apparently vomited several times before she died, not unusual in a drowning. What was unusual was that there were stomach contents under her fingernails. Drowning victims don't usually have the convenience of covering their mouths when they vomit. The second strange thing was that the water in her lungs had nowhere near the salt content of the water of the Atlantic, suggesting that there was fresh water in her lungs when she was placed in the ocean.

"You're not a suspect Branach, but we do need some answers from you," Trent finished.

"I'll be in tomorrow before the funeral. Thanks, Trent."

He hung up the phone without saying another word. And then I heard another "click." I placed the receiver back in the cradle then picked it up again. I dialed 411.

"3659012 Debbie, what city please?" The information operator asked in her machine-like tone.

"Hi Debbie," I said loudly. Then I heard the click again. "Debbie meet Deliah," I said. The information operator hung up and I heard Deliah slam down the receiver of her phone. I waited for her upstairs. Her footfalls were heavy even through the plush pile of the carpet on the stairs. I expected an argument, not a fight. She ran at me with her hands clenched together over her head. She swung down hard and her fists glanced off my left shoulder as I moved to avoid the blow. She whipped an opened backhand at me and the tip of the fingernail of her middle finger scratched my cheek. I caught her wrist as it went past me and I spun her around so that her back was against me. I clutched her in a bear hug as she bucked and kicked her feet out in front of her.

"Let me go dammit! Let me go!" she hollered.

"Why, so you can dig your nails into me? Calm down and I'll let you go." She struggled a moment longer and then turned into a rag doll in my arms. I helped her to the couch where she slumped into the cushions. Her sorrow and rage at her mother's death, and probably her father's as well, had been concentrated into one last ditch effort to hurt me. I probed my cheek and pulled back a few blood-stained fingers.

"You drew some blood if that makes you feel any better." She lifted her eyes toward me and I couldn't help but remember those eyes when they were in the head of her sociopathic father.

"I hate you Branach," she choked as tears began to flow. I knew she did. She had had ten years to blame me for the death of her father. And now she no doubt found me guilty of the murder of her mother.

"I understand." I said.

"No you don't. I don't hate you because of what happened with my father. I'm old enough now to realize that you saved my mother. I don't hate you for my mother's death, I hate you for my mother's life. You took advantage of her when she was virtually helpless and then you left her when she needed you most. That woman loved you, Thorpe. You fell back on the young and stupid angle and wrote it all off." She rolled over and buried her face in the pillows, crying like an eight-year-old whose mother just told her she wasn't old enough to get her ears pierced. I walked to the liquor cart and poured two fingers of vodka into a rocks glass. I rolled Deliah over and offered her the liquor.

"I don't really drink," she said as she took the glass. She sipped the vodka with one hand and pulled a crocheted afghan around herself with the other.

"Deliah," I said. "How did you get the safe opened?" She stopped sipping and then caught herself and continued.

"What are you talking about?" She looked up at me with feigned confusion.

"When the Golden Bean was stolen, you were house-sitting. Your mother said that she was the only one who knew the combination to the safe. When she returned, the necklace was gone." I studied her as she chewed the edge of the glass.

"You're crazy, Branach. And more heartless than I thought. My mother isn't even in the ground yet and you are here interrogating me." She began crying again, her face in her hands. I sat on the couch next to her.

"Look Deliah, the last thing your mother did was beg me to find this thing for her. The only explanation is that you got it out of the safe, or let somebody else do it. You talk about how I wrote your mother off. That's bull. I have been haunted by your mother every day of my life since I left Stone Harbor. I need to fulfill my promise to her that I would find the Golden Bean and then I need to let someone else into my life." She stopped crying and stood for the first time since her failed attack on me. As she walked to the liquor cart, I noticed a black rose tattoo on her left buttock showing through her sheer, white, silk pajamas. I wondered even more what type of person Deliah had been for the past ten years. A girl in the city with a murdered father and a jet-set mother. An attractive girl, angry at the world, can get herself into some deep, ugly trouble.

"I've been over this a million times Branach. Mom must have really believed you could find this thing and get it back. She was pretty much over you. I know she wouldn't have dragged up that horrible past unless she believed you could help. So be damn certain that I m not trusting you, I am trusting my mother." She swallowed a half-full glass of vodka. "But I need something from you. I need to know why my mother had such faith in you." She turned around and poured bourbon for a count of four into a fresh glass. She walked to me and handed me the glass. "I guess you could use this." I took the glass and the smell of the cola-brown liquid carried me back to New Orleans and the happy image of Adrian James. I sipped at the edge of the glass.

"Well Deliah," I said. "I'm fairly sure that your mother would have told you everything she knew about me. Why make me go through it again?" I could see the mental wheels turning behind her eyes.

"What I really want to know is, can you sense when things are getting dangerous?" I knew what she meant. The question indicated that she knew what it felt like when things got dangerous. I had been in situations where the skin grows clammy and cold and the world seems dark and small. It is at those moments when one knows what it was like when humans where just as much prey as predators. When night fell the loose bands of people huddled in caves and hoped that the wolves and lions would stay away. There is an instinct buried deep in the human DNA that allows one to sense when the wolves are closing in. To grasp the brief moment when escape or violence will save the species.

"I'm still breathing, kid," I said to Deliah as I sipped my drink. She seemed unconvinced. "Okay, you want drama?" I asked.

"Three years ago I was delivering a package to a law firm in Mexico City for a man in Florida. I succeeded in delivering the package but as soon as I left the building, four Federales grabbed me and tossed me into the back of a van. I was blind-folded and driven around for what seemed like hours. I could smell tequila and beer and marijuana smoke. Finally the van stopped and I was dragged out into a field. They removed the bandana that was blindfolding me and tied my wrists with it. They were all drunk and cursing at me in Spanish. All I could understand was 'Gringo.' Finally, one of them shoved me backward into a tree that stood alone in the clearing. He unsheathed a gleaming, steel hunting knife and held it in front of my face. I worked the knot in the bandana around my wrists which had become loose from the sweat pouring down my arms." Deliah's eyes were wide. She was sitting on the edge of the couch clutching a pillow between her knees and kneading it with her hands. I continued. "He lowered the knife and extended his arm straight out behind him. I knew the next move would bring the knife up into my gut. At that moment I got the knot undone. I caught his arm and used his momentum to twist him around and deliver the knife into his chest. As he fell, I snatched the rifle which was slung over his shoulder. It was an AK47 clone, and he had it set on full automatic with the safety off. His comrades were looking at me in confusion, as if I were a mirage created by the tequila and dope. I unloaded on them and watched them drop one by one. I then finished off the man who was going to kill me. They had driven me to a place where they knew no one would see or hear what they did to me. The same was true of what I did to them. I spent the next half hour loading the dead federales into the van. I drove until I found a road sign directing traffic toward Mexico City. Then I found a steep curve along a mountainside. I placed one of the Federales behind the wheel. Then I stuffed a torn shirt sleeve into the gas tank and lit it. I watched the van tumble over the cliff side. It rolled over and over hitting ragged outcroppings of rock. Finally there was gas spraying from the punctured tank as the van twisted in mid air. The liquid hit the flame and the entire mass erupted into a rolling fireball." Deliah slumped against the back of the couch. I walked over to the cart and freshened my drink. I finished the story as I turned back toward the couch. "I hitched a ride from two American kids who were on a six-month surfing tour of Latin America. I drove with them to Costa Rica then flew back to Miami." I sat next to her on the couch and breathed a heavy sigh. I leaned my head back and stared at the ceiling. Turning my head to the right, I looked at Deliah. I could see the question forming on her face.

"Why did they want to kill you?" she finally asked. I shifted to face her.

"When I got to Miami, I walked into the office of the man who gave me the package to deliver. He was surprised for just a split second. Then he said, 'Great, you're back in one piece.' During that split second of surprise, he told me through the expression on his face that he had set me up. He sent me to deliver a packet of documents detailing the merger of a United States concrete company with a Mexican counterpart. The insider information was worth millions to a few fatcat investors." Deliah yawned as the vodka began to take effect.

"I'm sorry, Thorpe," she said through the fist she had put to her mouth to cover the yawn. "I'm listening." I nodded.

"Well this is the most important part for you, Deliah. You see, I don't like the double cross. It rubs me the wrong way. I explained to the man in Miami that there is a certain person, in a certain part of the world who knows exactly where I am and exactly what I'm doing, and most importantly, for whom. If I die on the job, this person shows up to collect for me. If the employer won't pay off, things will get ugly." I watched her face as she pondered the possibilities. I sensed that Deliah was slick, but not smart. She knew how to manipulate and direct people, but she didn't really grasp the intricacies of the scam. She didn't know angles, just straight lines.

She was buying the Mexican story. Actually, it was Cuba, and I had delivered a package containing several hundred thousand American dollars to a Cuban business man at a time when it was still illegal to possess American currency in Cuba. I had gotten into Cuba on an Irish passport. On the night I tried to leave, I got into a scuffle with a cab driver who happened to be a Cuban Army Captain who was moonlighting. He pulled a gun and was going to arrest me, but I was able to knock him out and tie him up. I made my plane and got out before El Capitain woke up and got free. The embellishment that created the Mexican story seemed to fixate Deliah. I had had my share of excitement over the years. I had shot and been shot at. Deliah wanted excitement and danger, not a story of a clean, professional job. She didn't want to hear about preparation and intelligence and surveillance. She wanted Dirty Harry, so that's what I gave her.

"O.K. Deliah," I said. She twitched out of her zone

where she was reenacting the Federales going over the cliff. "I've given you something to think about, how about telling me everything you know." She leaned back against the couch and bit her lower lip. "I need to know what you did with that necklace after you got it out of the safe." I sipped my drink and never looked her in the eye. I watched her peripherally as her cheeks flushed and she dug her black-painted finger nails into the pillow on her lap.

"You think its that simple, huh Branach?" She stood up and faced me. "You think I took the Golden Bean and then got my mother killed. You son-of-a-bitch. If I thought I could have saved her life I would have." She was shouting now. I stood up and clutched her shoulders in my hands.

"Listen Deliah, I need to know. Its not about this necklace anymore. I want to find the people who killed your mother. Tell me everything. Now!" I released her and looked down into her eyes. The walls began to fall. She was realizing that she was now alone in the world. A murderous father killed while trying to do in a now-murdered mother. She was just Deliah now. No one to get attention from. No mother to impress or upset. Her world of calculated excess designed to gain her mother's attention was no longer relevant. She was adrift on a sea of loneliness and Thorpe Branach was the only lighthouse she could see.

She talked for an hour. Most of what she said meant little, but I let her go. This was the best kind of therapy she could get. Talk and talk and talk and dump all the emotional baggage. What was important was that she did have the combination to the safe. She did open the safe that night that her mother was away. She took the necklace out of the safe, but only to get at the stack of hundreds that her mother kept as petty cash. After getting a few hundreds to spend in Village clubs when she got back to New York, Deliah said she put the necklace back in the safe and locked it up. She had gotten the combination by leaving a little voice-activated tape recorder on the wall table by the safe. The tape recorder picked up each click of the combination. Deliah said it was easy. Of course when she got back to New York she had blabbed to her hipster friends about how she got into her mom's safe so that they could all drink four-dollar Rolling Rocks and eat five-dollar cheeseburgers. But the Golden Bean was supposedly gone the next day. There were two possibilities. One, Liza had checked the safe a few days after Deliah got into it and in the interim one of Deliah's friends had gotten the necklace out. Two, someone was with Deliah that night.

"So who was he?" I asked as Deliah finished talking. She fixed her eyes on mine and I could see the wheels turning again.

"Who was who?" She asked back, shrugging her shoulders and pressing her palms toward the ceiling. I moved close to her on the couch. She withdrew as far as she could and I moved closer.

"You know, Deliah, that there was someone here with you that night. You had a boyfriend down to Mom's beach house while she was away and he got a hold of the Golden Bean." She hugged the throw pillow and bit her lower lip. She couldn't look me in the eye. "If you don't want to tell me, that's fine," I said. "But I'm outta here if I can't get it all out of you. I've got better things to do." She was clutching the pillow and her lip looked as if it might burst under the pressure of her bite. I rose from the couch and walked to the sink in the kitchen. I found a clean dish towel and soaked in cold water from the tap. I rang it out and carried it over to Deliah.

"Lie down and put this on your forehead." She followed my instructions. "Now, when the room stops spinning and your ears stop ringing, you're going to tell me who he is, what he does, and why you let him get away with stealing the Golden Bean."

MICHAEL JOHN DONOHUE

-5-

I hadn't been to New York in a couple of years. In my courier days I spent a lot of time taxiing between Manhattan offices and New York airports, then flying off to all parts of the world to hand-deliver things that were sometimes too sensitive even to put in a diplomatic pouch. It was exciting and relatively safe and paid well. I was younger then and innocent. When a friendly man from the CIA suggested I might pad my wallet by carrying some packages for "The Company" on my delivery tours, I said "Sure." Before I knew it I was on flights and trips paid for entirely by the CIA. I was carrying packages to embassies and slum neighborhoods. The money was outrageous. They let me get shot at and when I was scared and feeling defenseless, they generously offered to take me to a little island in the Caribbean and teach me how to shoot and fight. In retrospect I can see all the tactics that they used to draw me deeper and deeper into the game without my even knowing it.

These were the same tactics that had been used by Vinny DeScarpa's family for a hundred years. The DeScarpa family had come through Ellis Island early. They had brought simple practices like protection and book-making to the tenements where they lived. These small-time grifts had turned into bootlegging and prostitution. Then the beautiful white powder from Columbia and Peru provided the DeScarpas with their most lucrative enterprise. Francesca DeScarpa, Vinny's mother, took over the reins of the Family after her husband was found in a Grand Central bathroom stall. His throat was slit and his tongue was pulled out through the opening. This is a Columbian necktie. Francesca assigned her eldest son Vincent, who at the time was just an overweight nightclub hound with a lot of hair on his back, to exact revenge on the Columbian gang that had infiltrated the neighborhoods. Vincent found that he had a knack for the work. He and four of his fellow hoods gave neck ties to eight different Columbian big-men over the course of two weeks.

When Deliah got done telling me the DeScarpa family history, I felt the draw of New Orleans and my Tulane Co-ed. Vinny was not someone I wanted to get to know. He was a scumbag, in legal parlance. Of course, chances were that Vinny was a big-mouthed airbag whose old man had had a heart attack while sitting on the head at Grand Central and whose mother was now running his life. But Deliah was cruelly playing Paul Harvey. She finally got to "the rest of the story."

"One day Vinny picked me up at my apartment in the village and said we were going to drive down to Atlantic City for the weekend. I told him that was great because my Mom was out of town and it was only another half-hour down to Stone Harbor. We got to Atlantic City and Vinny was walking around like a big man, people giving him hundred-dollar chips and bringing us drinks. You know, the good ones, not the watered-down ones. We gambled for a couple of hours and then Vinny said we had to go. We drove out to Brigantine to this little house. It was a little white house that looked like it should have been in some 1950's snapshot." I mixed myself a bourbon and coke while Deliah spoke. "I asked him who lived there and he wouldn't tell me. We went inside and there were four guys in suits sitting on the couch watching television. Vinny told me to have a seat. I told him I didn't want to stay, but he just walked through the house back to the kitchen. He didn't realize I was following him until we got to the kitchen doorway. In the split second that I was in the kitchen, I saw a Latin man tied to a kitchen chair. His nose was smashed against his face and he looked me right in the eye." She shuddered and pulled an afghan around herself. I could see the reflection of tears forming in the corners of her eyes.

"You don't have to tell me everything, Deliah. I think I've got enough." She shook her head from side to side and swallowed hard.

"No, Thorpe. I want you to believe me. I want to find out who did this to my mother and I know I can't do that without you." She stiffened her back and took a deep breath. "The man tied to the chair looked right into my eyes. His face was covered with blood, but his eyes were clear. His eyes were crying out to me. His eyes were asking me to save his life. His eyes knew that I was the only person in the house who cared whether he lived or died. Vinny shuffled me out of the house and made me sit in the car. I was crying and claustrophobic. Vinny came out of the house about twenty minutes later. He acted like nothing had happened. He said we were going down to Stone Harbor and that he couldn't wait to take a hot bath with me." She shuddered again. Then she got up and walked to kitchen sink. She filled a tall glass with water, drank the whole thing and then filled it again. I could see in her face, as she walked back to the house, that a great weight was lifting off her.

She had carried the Brigantine Latino around with her for a long time and now the image of the bloodied, longing man was finally beginning to fade. She continued.

"Needless to say I didn't let him near me. I let him spend the night, but the next morning I told him he had to leave. He kissed me on the cheek and said, 'I understand.' Then he left. I can still see the little smirk he wore as he walked out to his car." She sipped from the water glass. "He took it, Thorpe."

I sat up and focused on her, like a curious dog trying to hear a far off siren. "He told me he was going to hold onto it for a while, until he was sure I had forgotten what was going on in that little house outside of Atlantic City. I couldn't tell my mother. It would drag her into this mafia shit, too. I was just going to wait it out and then slip the Golden Bean back into the safe. It would be a mystery forever. But then I saw the ad in the New Yorker. Vinny was always flying down to Tampa. He'd come back all tan and happy. He said he was handling distribution for a cigar company. But one night when he was really hammered, he told me that he flew to Tampa to oversee marijuana shipments coming in from Mexico."

Deliah slumped back into the couch and took a deep breath. She exhaled forcefully, blowing the air out of her lungs toward the ceiling. I paced the room. Vinny DeScarpa got the Golden Bean. He knew it was valuable and that Deliah would want to get it back to her mother. But Vinny must have discovered how incredibly valuable the necklace actually was. The Golden Bean was beyond Vinny's worries about a little hipster NYU student making noises about a lowlife Columbian who had disappeared and whose remains would never be found. He was probably an illegal alien anyway. Vinny DeScarpa was shaping up as an above-average grifter. And he had made the king score when he stumbled across the Golden Bean.

I stood looking out through one of the panels of the big sliding-glass door that led to the beach-side deck. Lines of white foam rolled across the black Atlantic as sets of winter waves crashed to shore. It was a lonely and forbidding ocean. The look of it made me hope that Liza had died before they placed her in the water.

"I am such a goddamed idiot," Deliah said. I turned away from the window and saw her pounding her fist against her forehead.

"Deliah, I know you don't want to, but tell me a little more about Vinny. What's his style?" She stopped pounding herself and looked at me questioningly. "You know," I said. "How does he act when he's out in the clubs. His style." She rolled her eyes and clapped her hands.

"He's an ass. He walks into a place and kisses all the women and slaps all the men on the shoulder as he shakes their hands. And he tosses money everywhere. He tips the bartenders more than he pays for his drinks. He tips the doormen. He tips the D.J." She stopped talking suddenly. She looked into the distance, oblivious to the house, the room, me.

"Deliah, what is it?" She shook her head lightly and then directed her gaze at me.

"I only heard it once. It was the only family thing I ever went to with Vinny. It was a barbecue at his cousins or Uncle's or something. Anyway, this guy came up to Vinny and said, 'Hey, Mr. Green, long time.' Vinny smiled a nervous smile and looked at me. Then he leaned over to the guy and whispered something in his ear. They both smiled nervous smiles at me." Deliah looked at me as if to say, "Don't ya get it stupid?" For a moment I didn't get it. But then I remembered the New Yorker ad. Mr. Green was to be contacted in Tampa. It all fit.

"Deliah, you're going to New Orleans."

If everything was as Deliah described, and it did fit together nicely, then Deliah was more responsible for her mother's death then she could imagine. Deliah pieced together for me what she did for the few days before her mother's murder. She had moved among the basement speak-easys of Greenwich Village. Actually, they were the basement apartments of various NYU students and their friends. These neo-beatniks would spend days and nights, eating ecstasy and drinking expensive champagne, all the while whining about the lack of love they received from their rich parents. They would move from party to party, paying a fee at the door to cover the liquor and the drugs. The only thing they had in common with the original Beats was that most of them were either gay or neurotic or both.

It must have been during those days when Deliah and her hipster friends where practicing their particular form of 1990's escapism that Francesca DeScarpa decreed that the little NYU girl with the nice figure and the cold, dark eyes was to be processed into small pieces and scattered over the New Jersey Pine Barrens. When they couldn't find her in the city, they would have checked Liza's house. And it was there that a sadistic thug, desirous of impressing Francesca, gave Liza a choice: tell us where Deliah is, or drown. Liza didn't know where Deliah was. The safe was gone. The same stupid hood probably figured he'd take it as a gift to Vinny. The same stupid hood was probably himself driven to a little house outside of Atlantic City and then dumped somewhere, forever silent about his enormous blunder at the Jersey Shore.

I stayed in Stone Harbor, but Deliah left that night for New Orleans. She understood the danger she was in. She also understood that it would be more important to her mother that Deliah stay alive rather than make the funeral. She took my keys and I told her where I had the little snub-nosed .38 stashed in a hole in the boxspring of my bed. Somewhere in the back of my brain there was a little flea biting at the gray matter. He wasn't too annoying, but yet he was there. He was trying to tell me that maybe Deliah wasn't as lucky as she appeared. Maybe poor little Deliah and big, hairy Vinny were in it together. But then why drag Branach in? Why not just get rid of him? I decided to sleep, very lightly, on it. I had to meet Trent Roberts in the morning and convince him once and for all that I didn't know anything about Liza's death. Hopefully he wouldn't break out a polygraph.

* * *

I drove the rental car down Second Avenue to the Police Administration Building on 95th Street. The red brick facade was damp with morning dew. I walked up the concrete steps that I had climbed so many times ten years ago. I entered the building and found the dispatcher in a high, swivel chair, separated from me by a sheet of bullet-proof glass. A complicated panel of lights and switches had replaced the simple radio. She turned and asked if she could help me.

"I'm Thorpe Branach," I said. "I have an appointment with Trent Roberts." The dispatcher's disinterested gaze transformed into a questioning scowl.

"I'll get Lieutenant Roberts" she said as she got up from the chair. Trent was now a Lieutenant. No doubt he had spent a lot of time in training schools and gaining college credits. He jumped over a few of the old timers who probably resented him. But he was a good cop if nothing else. Stone Harbor law enforcement consisted mainly of driving around an empty town, waiting for summer when thirty thousand people would crowd into a three-mile space and celebrate. Trent was a patrolman ten years ago when I was mixed up in so much trouble. A gung-ho, sadistic sergeant named Makowski wanted to nail me to the wall for shooting Liza's husband. He tried to convince the Cape May County Prosecutor that I had planned the killing. That Liza had seduced me in order to bump off her ex-husband. Trent Roberts stuck his neck out. He stood up to Makowski and did some nice investigative work to put together a case which showed that Makowski was blowing hot-air and bucking for a jump up the chain of command. The prosecutor's office cleared me. Then I left Stone Harbor, and Liza, behind.

I heard the electronic buzzer and then Trent Roberts opened the door that lead to the interior of thc police station. He was older, and a few pounds heavier. He was in uniform and his belly was hanging ever so slightly over his gun belt.

"Morning, Branach, come on in." I followed Trent through the door and we walked up the steel stairs with vinyl traction-treads to where Trent has an office. I walked past him and he shut the door on the office.

"I'll get you outta here quick so you can get to the

funeral." He said as he rounded his desk and sat behind it. I scanned the walls and observed the various certificates and diplomas. FBI National Academy, Rutgers School of Criminology, N.J. State Police Academy-Municipal. The one I didn't expect was the Masters Degree in Criminal Justice from the University Of Oklahoma.

"Spent some time in Oklahoma, huh?" I asked. Trent swiveled in his chair and looked at the diploma.

"Nope. Actually never been there. I did all the work over the last five years on my computer. You tell people that and they think its a mail-order diploma. But it was tough and it cost me some bucks." There were four badges sitting on top of a filing cabinet beside the desk. It was traditional to frame your badges as you climbed up the ladder. It was the clearest example for the visitor that you had climbed the ladder and not gotten were you were by some back door. There was a price list for frames on Trent's desk. He had circled the shiny gold color with a red pen.

He swiveled back to face me. "Okay, Thorpe, I'm not gonna bullshit ya. There are a couple of people around here who really want to put you through the wringer on this. They think its too much that you show up here for the first time in ten years and all the sudden your lady friend turns up dead. We know that you were in New Orleans when this murder took place. We know that for certain because guess who saw you at the airport in Philly?" He smiled.

"Who?" I asked quickly. Trent swiveled back and forth in his leather Captain's chair.

"Makowski." He smiled again. "You believe it? Makowski is now a security guard at the Philadelphia International Airport and when we started asking around up there to see if you actually left town. Makowski confirmed it. Along with the gate crew. Ironical, don't ya think?" I shook my head in amazement.

"Yeah," I said. Then Trent's face hardened.

"You have to tell me why you were in town and exactly what you and the lady talked about, and I have to believe you before we cut you loose."

I hadn't slept the night before. I had come up with several stories and then I concentrated on the one that I thought was the most believable. I repeated it over and over again to myself for hours. A polygraph test works by measuring changes in certain physical reactions. The operator asks you a few questions that he knows you can't lie about, "Is your name Thorpe Branach? Are you a Caucasian male? Are you six-foot-four?" This way they get some standards to judge when you're lying. But if you truly believe what you're saying, the machine will tell the operator that you're telling the truth. It's actually a form of hypnosis. You tell yourself the story over and over and each time you tell yourself that it is absolutely true. If you can stick with it long enough, your body believes that it's true and physiologically, you tell the machine that you're telling the truth.

"Why don't you hook me up and I'll answer all the questions. That way we can put this to rest for good." Trent sighed.

"Well, just tell me the story first. We got a few minutes

before the guy gets here with the machine." Trent had already planned for the polygraph. I was happy I had spent the night sleepless.

Cops are used to being lied to. They deal always with people who make a living by deception. Even a man who is driving so drunk that a vampire would be over the legal limit after just a sip of his blood will tell the cop that pulls him over that he only had two beers. A cop can watch someone break into the cop's own car and then listen to the story of how the car belongs to the robber's friend and he thought he locked the keys inside. I had to come up with a story that was not only believable, but a story that a cop would believe.

Essentially, I told the truth. Only I replaced the search for the Golden Bean with a sheet of photographic negatives. I told Trent that Liza had gotten herself into a rather indiscrete situation over in Europe and that her partner in the tango had set her up. There were thirty-six photos of Liza and the man in various positions. He wanted ten grand for the negatives. I told Trent that I had gotten a package from Liza. It contained a letter explaining her problem, which I had of course destroyed, and ten thousand dollars in hundred dollar bills. This was in January. I flew to Paris, where I met a woman who took the money and gave me the negatives. He could check the flight records and find my reservations. Luckily for me, I had gone to Paris at that time for a friend's wedding, but Trent wouldn't go so far as to check what I did over there. A short time ago I got another letter from Liza. She wanted me to come to Stone Harbor because she had gotten another photo in the mail. On the back of it was typed, "Now $10K for the prints." I flew up, told her that there could be a hundred copies of the picture and that unless she was prepared to pay ten thousand bucks every couple of months, she should get over it. She was a consenting adult with no husband, who could do whatever she wanted. I told her to please not contact me again and I left the next day.

The story was part truth, part fantasy, but it satisfied the cop's eye. It was believable. It had a little sex mixed in and it was something to share with the boys. That was the key. After I had left and Trent was sitting around with the troops, the male officers of course, he would have a great story to tell about the dead beautiful woman that they had all coveted for so long. He wanted the story to be true. He would eliminate the blackmailers as suspects quite easily. The motive wasn't there. These people were European scumbags hidden in some Paris backstreet. There was no reason for them to come to New Jersey to torture Liza to death. Trent believed me. He was satisfied that there was something in that safe that the murderer wanted. He tried to drown the combination out of Liza but she died too fast. For Trent Roberts, what was in the safe was the key to the whole mystery. How right he was. He bought my story and he asked me if I had any ideas about who might have done it. I told him I didn't know anything about the safe or what might have been in it. I hadn't spoken to Liza outside of the Paris problem, in ten years. Liza knew a lot of people in a lot of places. I wished him good luck. Thank God he believed me. But more importantly, the machine believed me too.

-7-

Mob angles are a little different from other angles. When you have the luxury of a system that allows you to systematically murder and dispose of people, risk is significantly lowered. In business and government, most people don't go so far as to kill a person who is standing in the way of their deal. They negotiate. They change the figures. They use different angles because they have to play by different rules. There was once an apartment in New York City where the New York mob sent bodies for processing. It was like a stolen car chop-shop. The dead would be drained of liquid, taken apart and shipped out. Maybe they'd be ground-up and spread over the Everglades in Florida. Maybe they'd be reduced to liquid in vats of hydrochloric acid, placed in fifty-gallon drums and dumped at sea. Whatever the method, they were gotten rid of. There were few people that the mob would not dispose of in this way. A family member who had no hands-on involvement in the business. A priest. And a cop. If you had to kill a cop you better make damned sure the reason is right and that the cop disappears without a trace. You might try to set him up with a hooker or with some drugs and get some pictures. That gives him a motive to disappear. You kill a cop any other way and there is a bonafide war. The police are underfunded, undermanned, and hamstrung by the Constitution. But kill one of their own and they will drop everything else until they get you. That's not good for business.

There were several times as I drove back to Liza's

house, that I almost turned around and drove back to the police station. I would tell Trent the truth. Let him go to work, then go back to New Orleans and forget about it. But there was too much at stake. For a Stone Harbor cop to actually find and prosecute these people would be astronomical. They would throw up walls everywhere. They would get witnesses out of the country. They would have the best lawyers in New York creating legal obstacle courses that would deplete all resources. They would also lose the Golden Bean for good. I wanted it. I wanted it because it belonged to Liza. She was dead and gone, but for so long she had been such a huge part of my life. I had saved her once. If I hadn't been in such a hurry to get away from her, I might have been there when they showed up. I might have saved her again. Justice sometimes should avoid law enforcement. Very often the two are incompatible. Vinny DeScarpa would have to be gotten on his own turf in a game played by his rules. The plan wasn't quite clear yet, but it had something to do with the big trust fund Deliah said she would get out of Liza's estate, and maybe the Detective's badge I lifted from Trent's office.

* * *

There is something about a funeral that makes me strangely giddy. I think my mind is so absolutely incapable of grasping exactly what is going on, that it short circuits and I'm left numb and feeling a little drunk. It's a defense system that kicks in during times of metaphysical crisis. Where was she now? Was her soul left in perpetual torment because of the way she died? Had she actually been a horrible person at heart and was now trapped in the eternal torment of hell? I suspected not. I suspected that Liza was an angel of the highest order. In life she was one of the masses of women who have been trapped and abused by men. She was one of the scarred and scared. Trust was a difficult thing for her and she had placed that trust in me.

There were a few people at the funeral. I didn't know any of them and none of them knew me. Trent Robert's subordinates stood on the periphery, dressed in plain clothes. I knew that somewhere there was a detective focusing a camera with a long lens. He would take everyone's picture and he and Trent would find out who each one was and what the connection was to Liza. Trent had grilled Deliah, subtly of course, prior to my arrival, and was satisfied that she was not involved. Deliah was apparently a skilled liar. That scared me. I tossed a flower into the hole. It landed on top of the casket, then bounced and slid off the side where I lost sight of it. I walked back to my car and set off for the airport.

As I drove west on the Atlantic City Expressway, I imagined Vinny DeScarpa, making his plans on how to spend the millions he was going to make off the Golden Bean. But there was something else making him anxious. Deliah. She was on the loose. Perhaps Vinny had watched the funeral from afar, hoping to see Deliah and snatch her away. Now he was caught between his lust for cash and his fear that his NYU girl might be able to give the cops a few details about the DeScarpa's. But Mr. Green was undoubtedly getting calls in Tampa and the sale of the necklace couldn't be far away. Vinny was juggling two very important priorities. First, he had to keep the necklace sale as quiet as possible within his circle of marijuana connections. Second, he had to satisfy Francesca that the Deliah problem was being taken care of. As I analyzed Vinny DeScarpa over and over again, I begin to see a few twists in the angles. He had trusted Deliah, presumably because she was performing certain services for him which he enjoyed. He had misjudged the character of the hood he sent to Liza's house. There was nothing to be gained by killing Liza. It must have been a bungled job. These are the tragic flaws of men placed in positions of power. They can't keep their pants on and they can't judge character. They hunt trophy women and they choose bootlicking sycophants as their stooges. These were the weaknesses Vinny possessed. The plan was beginning to take on sharper focus.

-8-

I returned the rental car and walked to the American Airlines ticket gate. They credited my return ticket to New Orleans toward a round-trip ticket to Dominica in the Caribbean.

He was there, as he always is. I met him several years ago. The Company had me posing as a computer salesman in Columbia. I carried high-tech samples in and then the D.E.A. tracked the hardware straight into the haciendas of the leaders of the Medellian cartel. I had flown out of Caracas, Venezuela to the island of Dominica. Dominica is considered the jewel of the Caribbean. There are mountains high enough to pierce the clouds. There are boiling lakes heated by the core of the Earth itself. I had spent a week on Dominica and then I got a call to meet a man at a small bar in the harbor. It was the type of call I got more and more often as I spiralled deeper into the well of involvement with the CIA. Riding a moped along the steep, winding roadways of the island, I lost myself in the glamour of my life. I was young, strong and living on the edge, albeit the safe side of the edge.

The bar was typical of the Caribbean. The roof was corrugated aluminum, blistered with oxidation. There were wide windows with broad shutters. The shudders where painted red probably twenty years earlier. The paint was now cracked and peeling. The shudders were wide open, and three ceiling fans stirred the cigar smoke of the few men and women who were drinking and playing pool in the hot afternoon. I walked in and bought a longneck

Budwieser. The beer was ice cold and the bottle sweated in my hand. I turned and leaned my back against the bar. Sipping the beer, I surveyed the clientele. No one made eye contact with me. Usually the cloak and dagger act was minimal. I would meet a respectable looking man or woman who would give me a package and tell me where to take it, or tell me where to go to pick something up. But no one in the bar fit the mode. They were all older, fifties, sixties. They were the typical ethnic mix of Native West Indian, African and various European blood. The mix had created a beautiful people. But overall there is a Latin look to the modern inhabitants of the Caribbean. That's why I missed him. He blended in so well. When I turned back to the bartender to order another beer, I found one waiting and the bartender smiling.

"Tis on him suh," the bartender said as he nodded toward an old man sitting on the edge of the one pool table that wasn't in use. He was watching the game at the next table, swinging his feet as he smiled and sarcastically critiqued each player's shot. I stood at the bar for a moment and then walked to the back of the room and sat against the wall at a small wooden table. He hopped to his feet and, without looking at me, walked to the bar and bought two more beers. He walked to my table and sat across from me. It wasn't until he was sitting three feet from me that I realized how old he was. He was seventy if he was a day. He made me nervous.

"Don't worry kid," he said. I detected an Italian-American accent poking through the West Indian influence on his speech. "I'm here to help." I was convinced that he was not with the Company. I had gotten in deep enough to believe that if you weren't on our side you were on the wrong side.

"I didn't realize I needed any help," I said, sticking out my jaw and then sipping my beer. He smiled.

"You are right. You don't realize." Then he began to talk. He was in Cuba early under Batista. He set up a Casino for the New York families while Castro was just a college student in America. But he was a businessman. He engaged in no practice other than running a Casino. He made crates full of money for himself and for the families. Then a young Yankee pitching prospect got cut and decided to go home and overthrow the local dictator. Castro came in and in no time was targeting the mob in Cuba. He said they were tools of an American Imperialist regime.

"Another beer?" he paused to ask. The heat of the afternoon was pumping the alcohol through my body quickly. I asked for a coke. He nodded and smiled then walked to the bar. I was more confused now. So what, I thought. What does this have to do with me? What's the point? He returned with my coke and his beer and continued his story. He hung on in Cuba as long as he could and was about to pack it in when he was approached by an old family friend from New York.

"'Hang in there', they told me. 'We're gonna take this guy out.' I hung in there. They showed up one night and I had orders to take care of them." Four men showed up with long metal cases. He put them up for the night and they left the next day. Then a man showed up and said he was from the CIA.

"He told me to come with him. We went out to an airstrip cut into the rainforest and we flew to Miami. I spent the next six years working for the families and for the Company. I was grateful, I was young and it was exciting. Then someone pushing papers across a desk somewhere decided that I was a track that needed to be covered. They came for me, kid. They would have got me too, except the guy they sent could have passed for me. He was my size, my build. Didn't really look like me, but from a distance, maybe." He pulled a bandana from the back pocket of his khaki shorts and wiped the sweat from his brow. "He missed me with the first shot and he had gotten too close. I got the gun and when he pulled another one from his sock, I let him have it. It was the first really criminal type thing I had ever done. At first I thought it was something in the family. But that wasn't it. This was government work. They send a guy out to kill somebody, then the killer disappears, forever. One hit, then gone. It works so well that it's moved from the government to the private sector from what I hear." The story continued. He shot the man in the face with the seven bullets that were left in the nine-millimeter handgun. There was no face or dental work or much bone structure left. Then he traded clothes with the dead killer.

"That is how I ended up in paradise. I guess you could say I died and went to heaven that day. Of course, when I first came down here this place wasn't much changed since the time Columbus buzzed past here." I studied him. He acted like he knew me. Like I was some familiar nephew who needed advice.

"That's an interesting story, sir," I said. "But what's it got to do with me?" He smiled again.

"Last year. The little Italian girl." He saw the recognition of remembrance move across my face. "Ah, you remember. You pig." He studied me for a second then shrugged his shoulders. "Ah, we all adore beautiful women. Only this one happened to be my niece. She and my sister are the only two people in the world who know who I am. Well, one of three now. Here's the point, kid. I checked you out because my beautiful niece was hung-up on you. I've made lots of connections in lots of different places. I haven't just been a sump down here, you know. I even got a friend who works for the Company. Strange world, huh? Anyway, I thought I might invite you back one time when she's here." He sipped his beer and wiped his brow again. "But I found out some things about you that I didn't like. Of course the niece is out of the picture. Then I got to thinking. This is me. This is me forty years ago. I'm old, kid. I'm a prisoner even though this place is like Eden. I want to do something that I can take to the bank upstairs."

By the time the sun set, I was convinced that it was time to get out of CIA contract work. So I went to New Orleans and started college again. I told the men and women who called that I was now just a student and that I just wanted to be normal again. I lived in fear of the faceless killer they would send for me. But he never came. Eventually the feelings passed. But I got bored. I found a market out there of people who have lost things, or need to get things somewhere or out of somewhere. It was the same work that I did for the Company, but it was private sector and much safer. I never worked for the same employer twice. It was all pretty much gravy until Liza jumped back into my life.

Now here I was back in Dominica, sitting across the same table from my old, wise friend. He had aged a bit more. His energy had diminished. But he was still sharp.

"I don't think I've seen you look this worried since we first met years back," he said. He was drinking water from a tall, plastic glass. "Start from the beginning and just keep talking. I got nowhere to go." I told him the entire story. I started with the day Liza and I had first met ten years ago in Stone Harbor. After an hour or so, I finished with the fact that Deliah was now at my place in New Orleans.

"Whew!" he said, then wiped his brow with the ever-present bandana. "Lets walk by the water." I helped him up from his chair. We walked out of the bar.

"How do you like the new paint job?" The shutters where bright red and the wooden sides of the building were powder blue.

"Needs a new roof," I said.

"Ah, there's that Thorpe Branach humor I've come to know and hate." We laughed for a moment as we rounded the corner and made our way along the waterfront. The Caribbean stretched out in its Marian blue, streaked with the fire orange and pink of the setting sun. The laughter turned serious as he tried to convince me to turn Deliah over to the F.B.I. and get out of the country for a while. I couldn't, and he knew why. Vinny DeScarpa would never suffer in any way. He would walk away with the cash and never be linked to anything but a Columbian illegal who was gone and whom no one had reported missing.

"You may not believe it, Thorpe, but it would be easier for you to tangle with the Company rather than butt heads with these guys." I skipped a rock across the water and watched the rings rippling out from each spot where the rock had skipped.

"These are big-time bad people. The business has changed. It got dirty when all this cocaine money started flowing. Now you've got respectable families in bed with these crazy Latinos. Its all about killing now. There is no other weapon with these people. They kill for things that used to be laughed off. So we gotta kill back." He stopped walking and looked me in the eyes. "Branach, you better be ready, 'cause the other guy is. He'll make sure you're dead and he won't have to make it look like an accident because you'll be gone for good." I stared at my feet for a moment.

"Look," I said. "I know you've got the inside track to how these people operate, but aren't you speaking in generalities? I mean, we're talking about a second rate, spoiled brat who's trying to free-lance his way into some big time cash." He thought for a moment, rubbing his chin.

"Well Thorpe, let me just say this. Some of the most despicable men in history, and in the history of the Families, were low-lifes. They were little men who for years were beaten down. Then one day they get a hold of a little power and they're killing people. Sometimes lots of people." He was right. I thought of all the little men who had become big-time killers. Of course there was Hitler foremost among them all. Then there was Jimmy Randal. I knew him in grade school. He was a class "A" nerd and everyone treated him as such. It was the same story in high school, only Jimmy started to lose his sense of humor about it. He became less self effacing. I saw him eight years after high school in New York. He was working on Wall Street making tons of dough. He had the best of everything. But behind closed doors, Jimmy was taking out a lifetime of frustration on the young women he picked up with his money. They are all over, the young, pretty girls with dollar signs in their hearts. Jimmy did some nasty things. He probably would have become the Wall Street Mass Murderer, only one of the girls actually had the guts to go to the police. She testified to all of it. She went through the humiliation all over again and she put Jimmy away. She saved lives. I suspected Vinny DeScarpa fit the Jimmy Randal mold. He was a spoiled little butterball as a kid. He didn't fit in with other teenagers because of his family name. But as soon as Vinny entered the part of his life where he was expected to be a man, he blossomed into an animal. He was the perfect vehicle for Deliah to use to get back at her shattered life.

"He won't stop looking for her will he?" I asked.

"No. He'll put a lot of people on it. She's not just privy to the little house in Brigantine, she's muckin' up his necklace deal. I don't know any DeScarpa kids. They got in the powder market early. A lot of the families wrote them off, but in hindsight, they led the way. The best you can hope for is that he is flying solo on the necklace thing.

If he is, his resources will be more limited. But he'll still be trying his best to tie up this loose end." We walked back to the bar. There were five or six Navy seamen flocking like seagulls around a beautiful, young Dominican girl who was sitting at the bar sipping a rum tonic. The night crowd was starting to gather.

"You wanna beer, Thorpe?" I said yes and walked to an empty table. He approached with the beers and sat across from me. "Okay, I don't like it, but I understand. You gotta do whatcha gotta do. I'll give you all the help I can kid, but it might not be much." He sipped the beer.

"I don't really know what I'm going to do just yet. I might need to bounce some ideas off you though. That's all I'm asking." He nodded and drank some more from the bottle.

"I'm gonna do one thing for you kid. Its something that I shouldn't do. Its a last resort." He pulled a pen from the apron of a passing waitress and scrawled a phone number on a napkin. "You find yourself with no way out you call this number. You ask for Michael Graziano and you tell him this, 'Viva el Cubano!'" I almost laughed at this scenario. But the seriousness in his face made mc realize how real all this was.

"Viva el Cubano?" I asked.

"That's right kid. This might blow the lid off my long exile here, but if its the difference between you gettin' outta some deep trouble or you being fertilizer in the everglades, I'll take that chance. Graziano is the son of my late best friend. I practically raised Michael when his father died young of a heart attack. I was The Cubano. When the heat was on, I put Michael on a plane out of Cuba and I told him not to worry, The Cubano would ride again. That was the last time I saw him." He looked at his watch. "I'm gonna get home, Thorpe. You stay," he said as he rose from his chair. He turned and looked toward the door then looked at his watch again. "There should be somebody here soon to help you finish that beer. Ah, yes." He raised his arms and embraced a strikingly gorgeous, young Italian woman. It was Stephania, The Cubano's niece with whom I had spent an interesting week many years ago.

"Stephania, I believe you know Mr. Branach." I stood and leaned across the table to take her hand. She smiled and eased herself into the chair her uncle had just vacated. Her olive skin was still flawless, although a few crow's feet were starting to form at the corners of her brilliant green eyes. I felt a slight tremble in her small hand.

"Hello, Stephania," I said finally. The Cubano smiled and gave me a thumbs up as he walked toward the door. I refocused on Stephania. She was wearing a black, short sleeve, silk shirt and faded blue jeans. Her long black hair melted into the blackness of her shirt as it flowed onto her shoulders. She wore a slight smile that parted her lips just enough to reveal the smooth edge of her teeth.

"How have you been Thorpe?" It was the opening question in what was to be an evening of harmless questions and small talk. We drank beer and ate roast pork and blackbeans and rice.

"I'm glad we got this time to talk, Thorpe," Stephania said as I reached into my shorts pocket to pay the bill. "I wondered what ever became of you. My Uncle hasn't spoken of you in a long time." I put the money on the table and placed an empty beer bottle on top of it. We rose form our seats, walked through the bar and out into the warm Caribbean night.

"I wish I could come down here more often," I said as we walked to the waterfront and stared across the dark sea. "I wish I could just toss it all and stay here." Stephania wrapped her left arm around my waist and I lifted my right arm over her head and took her shoulder in my hand. She tucked her head below my chin against my chest.

"It is a beautiful place. But I think it could get lonely. I know my Uncle would prefer to have lived a normal life rather than end up in exile down here." She looked up at me and smiled. "Well, its time for you to give me a ride home on the back of your little moped. I took a taxi into town." We looked into each other's eyes and seemed to hang there in a moment of time that went on and on. When it was over, we did not kiss. Whatever part of the brain that makes those split-second, emotional decisions had decided against opening that particular can of worms.

As we rode along the dark, winding roads, Stephania held me tight around the waist. The wind was warm and heavy with the smell of the lush flora of the island mixed with the gas fumes from the moped's engine. I pulled into the long, gravel driveway that led to The Cubano's one story Caribbean estate. Stephania dismounted and walked to the front of the moped. The beam from the headlight turned her into a silhouette with a shadow stretching behind for a hundred feet. I flipped the switch and turned off the light.

"I'm leaving in the morning for New York, but I'll be back here in the fall for a month's stay," Stephania said. She was swaying and she nervously gave the front tire a gentle kick.

"Maybe I can make it back then," I said. She smiled and walked over to me.

"Maybe?" She asked. "It'll probably be another couple of years before I see you again, Branach. I guess I should have kissed you when I had the chance." I held out my hand and she took it. I pulled her toward me. She gave me a quick peck on the cheek and took a step back.

"No," she said simply. "I think we made the right decision." I nodded in agreement and gave the moped some gas. The back tire slid a bit on the gravel then gained traction and I was heading down the driveway.

"Thorpe?" I heard Stephania shout behind me. I stopped and looked over my shoulder. "Maybe?" She shouted. I laughed.

"Maybe!" I shouted back. She smiled and stood on her tip-toes and waved her hand excitedly above her head. I returned the wave and headed back down the driveway and to my rented cottage by the beach.

* * *

I lay on a chaise lounge listening to the gentle Caribbean waves roll over the reef a few hundred yards off the beach. The wind was coming off the water in gentle, warm gusts. I looked out across the dark sea and thought of New Orleans up there, moving to its city beat. I thought of sleepy Stone Harbor, waiting for the tide of tourists to come flocking back. For a moment I was calm and happy to be so far away. But then I thought of Liza in a metal box in the cold, late-winter ground. It was all over for her. She wasn't confused about what to do next. She wasn't afraid of walking into a violent and unpredictable world. She was out of it. But I knew that she would much rather have stayed in it. To see her daughter grow out of her extended adolescence. To get her necklace back and live an easy and comfortable last thirty years. It struck me, as I listened to the lapping water, that it was over for me as well. I no longer had to find a way to deal with Liza. It was not a problem any more to wonder how she was coping, if she still thought of those old days. I was free of her and I felt a sick relief. She was dead, tortured, and I was feeling relieved. There was a horrible emotional conflict going on in my mind that made me want to drive back to The Cubano's and tell Stephania I'd be waiting when she got back.

I pulled off my shirt and walked to the water's edge. Wading in, I stirred up the naturally phosphorescent algaes that were drifting at the whim of the current. The little green lights mimicked the dotted, starry sky. I waded out to chest depth and leaned back, letting my feet rise in front of me. I bobbed in the salty water of the Caribbean and stared at the speckled sky. I was weightless and tranquil. The thought occurred to me that Liza was probably in a quite similar condition. She was probably up there among those stars, floating and gazing down on the earth. My guilt subsided as I reached the conclusion that its not so horrible to be relieved when someone dies. When you realize that someone has escaped this grueling trial we call life, you can't help but feel relieved. I floated there until I felt myself drifting away. The world fell away from me and I was simply adrift. I felt nothing and saw only stars and blackness. Then a school of fry passed under me and brushed against me like a hundred-fingered hand. It startled me out of my trance.

I made my way to shore and walked back to my cottage. There I spent a restless night with dreams of wolves and water. I had the dream where the legs won't work but I have to run. I had the dream where I'm trapped in a car that has crashed off a bridge and I'm sinking fast. But it was the wolf dream that I feared the most. A lone wolf appears at the edge of a field in which I'm standing. I look for others and there are none. I decide to run but every new direction brings a new wolf. But its the same wolf. Dark, almost black, fur with steely, cold, powder-blue eyes. He is everywhere and there is no way out for me until I awake in a pool of sweat, my heart pounding, my throat as dry as dust. I knew the dream would be back every night until the wolf had killed me, or I him.

MICHAEL JOHN DONOHUE

-9-

I flew into New Orleans where the mid-day sun was evaporating a morning rain from the streets and sidewalks. I took a cab into the French Quarter, and climbed out in front of the Cafe Du Monde. An ancient Black man stood with his back to the black, wrought-iron railing running down the side of the Cafe. His saxophone case was battered and worn. It was open by his feet. The sax didn't wail or moan. The sound eased out of it and floated on the air like the smell of honeysuckle. The notes were deep and full and spoke of wasted years and lost love. I reached in my pocket and pulled out all the loose change I had. I tossed in every coin except for one quarter. I couldn't decide if I wanted to eat coffee and beignets or beer and crawfish, so I decided to flip for it. I flipped the quarter. Tails for crawdad. It was tails.

I hurried across the street against the light and walked through Jackson Square. The bells of the St. Louis Cathedral were ringing as a novice student ringer practiced inside. I made my way down Canal Street to Le Rondule. They had the best crawdad in the Quarter and I ate about a hundred of them. I washed the spicy juice down with some Jax beer then walked out of the Quarter to the streetcar stop. There were a few tourists holding shopping bags, craning there necks to look down the street as if they could conjure the streetcar out of thin air. Finally, the tracks began to rattle and I could hear the overhead contact scraping along the power line that energized the car. The streetcar rounded the corner and I felt oddly at ease at the sight of its green sides and wooden seats. I stepped on board and sat next to an open window. The streetcar clacked its way up St. Charles Avenue, under the budding oaks and deposited me on the far side of the Garden District. My studio apartment was a block off St. Charles on the third floor of an eighteenth century house that allegedly housed some vacationing Napoleons at some point.

As I climbed the stairs I ran through the upcoming scene in my mind. I would try to convince Deliah that she had to give me a whole lot of money so that I could show up at the auction of the Golden Bean and convince the scumbag auctioneer that I was legitimately, disgustingly rich. I fumbled through my backpack and found my keys. I had instructed Deliah to not answer the door.

There weren't any emptied-out and tumbled drawers, the cushions weren't slashed and scattered about the room. There was just a simple note in the middle of the small table where I piled my books and ate my dinner.

"We got the girl. You got the necklace. We'll be in touch." I had no idea how long the note had been there. I was feeling confused and spastic. I could hear my breath quickening and feel my heart pump. My eyes fixed on the answering machine and its blinking little red light. I leaped toward it and poked at the playback button. It clicked and beeped and I heard messages from various friends regarding things that once seemed very important. Parties, concerts, job opportunities. But no New York accent. Of course not. People who fear the law, know the law. An answering machine tape is potential evidence of a crime.

My mind was racing. No Deliah. No necklace. No element of surprise anymore.

I slumped into the couch and tried to catch my breath. Closing my eyes was a bad idea. The image of Vinny trying to coax some information out of his old girlfriend was rolling on the personal viewing screen of my mind. I pushed myself up off the couch and heard footfalls on the stairs. I tiptoed quickly to the bedside and reached between the mattress and boxspring. My little snub-nosed .38 was there, just where I had told Deliah to keep it. I drew it out and stood along side the door as the sound of a person walking echoed in the stairwell. The sound grew louder then stopped outside my door. I flipped a coin in my mind to decide whether to run for the fire escape or yank the door open and lead with the .38.

The door felt like it was made of balsa as my adrenalin induced muscles gained strength and power. I flung it open, stepped back and leveled the gun at the mid-section of a startled Deliah, who dropped a brown bag containing a dozen eggs, a tub of ricotta cheese and a bottle of marinara sauce which shattered along with the eggs.

"What the fu..." I yanked her inside the apartment before she could finish and slammed the door shut. "Nice to see you too, Branach," she said, as she tried to get back out into the hallway and collect her groceries.

"Don't open the door, Deliah." I shoved her toward the couch then walked around and pulled all the window shades.

"What the hell is going on, Thorpe?" I finally paused in the middle of the room and composed myself.

"Here," I said as I picked up the note and handed it to her. A look came over her face like that of a little kid who has broken something he shouldn't have been playing with and now is going to cry as he confesses. Then it struck me.

"Was Rocky here?" I asked quietly. Deliah cocked her head in confusion.

"Who?" she asked.

"Rocky!" I shouted. "Was she here?" Deliah sat there dumbly. I grabbed her shoulders in my hands. "Adrian. Was there a girl here named Adrian?" Her face quivered and tears began to stream down her cheeks. I pushed her back toward the couch and she fell onto her rump about a foot short of the cushions thumping onto the hardwood floor.

"Yes," she said. "She kept coming to the door, so I finally let her in. She's a nice girl, Thorpe. I needed some company and she was fun to hang out with. All she talked about was you and how worried she was about you."

I was desperate now. I could hear my blood rushing through me. My world turned on an angle and I clung to the side of the table for balance. This had gotten all messed up. I was supposed to be able to throw somebody else's money around and act like a big shot and take away a big chunk of the scam. This was new territory.

"Oh, that'll help." Deliah said as I pulled a bottle of Jim Beam out of the antique china closet.

"Shut-up," was all I said before I took a long swallow from the bottle. The liquid lightening zapped through my body, slowed my heart and rattled some of the bugs out of my brain. I felt the pull of that feeling, the escape it offered, but I couldn't go there. I put it back in the cabinet. My only option was to sit and wait. Maybe Vinny would call or maybe he would send someone over to take care of Branach, the only loose end left. Either way I would do my best to play the hand he dealt. But I needed some info.

"What are you doing?" Deliah shouted as I took her by the arm and hauled her off toward the bathroom.

"See that?" I said.

"What? The tub?"

"Yes the tub. They dunked your mother into her tub so many times that she drowned in her own house." I felt her body slacken then tighten as she swung her free fist at my face. I let her hit me. The blow caught me above the left eye brow. It undoubtedly hurt her fist more than my head. She slammed down the toilet lid and sat there rubbing her hand, shaking it occasionally as if it were wet. "Your mother is dead and now someone that I care very much about is in serious trouble, Deliah. You better come clean right now or I'm going to use you as a bargaining chip in this thing." I'm certain she saw the sincerity in my eyes. She was no longer a tragic figure to me. Her mother was dead because of her. Now Deliah was responsible for sending Rocky into a world as foreign to her as if she had awoke on Mars. I sat on the edge of the tub and stared at her. She got up and walked out of the bathroom. By the time I caught up with her, she had a bottle of vodka out of the cabinet and was headed for the kitchen counter where inverted glasses where drying on a dish towel.

"Thorpe, I only left here an hour ago. This must have just happened." She poured herself a glassful and then took ice cubes from the freezer. I had realized what Deliah was saying but didn't want to think about it. The "ifs" were creeping in. If only I hadn't stopped to eat. If only I had left Dominica a day earlier. If only. But the "ifs" weren't going to resolve the problems. Deliah had to tell it all. She did.

-10-

I should have calmed myself down before I settled into my old, oak rocking chair to baby-sit the phone. I was there for the next three days. I would rise occasionally to eat or drink or get rid of what I ate or drank. Occasionally a friend would call and I'd ask her not to call again for a few days and to let everyone know the same. The little, white, cordless phone became the image that controlled my thoughts. I would dose off and dream of it ringing, only to find it sleeping contentedly in its cradle when I awoke. It seems to me that sound waves may reach the ear and cause a reaction in the brain before the sound is ever heard. I jumped awake spastically in the rocker and reached for my gun. Finally, the ringing of the phone was clear and loud. My mouth went dry and my throat closed up. My palms began to sweat. Three days of adrenaline intensity had led to this moment. I hoped it was someone who hadn't gotten the message to not call Branach. But I knew it wasn't. Deliah walked out from the bedroom, her eyes full of anxiety. Urging me with her expression to answer it. I picked up the receiver and poked the "talk" button. I listen to the electric hiss of the connection.

"You there?" a tinny, high voice came across the line. It sounded like a young man who smoked too many cigarettes.

"Who's this?" I asked, as calmly as I could.

"You don't need to know that. I know you're Branach and that you were in Stone Harbor not too long ago. You get around. You got something we want and we got something you want." I let the caller's words linger. I had to pick a plan of the many I had formulated over the past three days.

"Why the hell have you kidnapped my french tutor?" The line was silent. I had hoped Vinny would assign some expendable lacky to do his dirty work over the phone. Perhaps he had. "Who are you? That girl hasn't taken anything from anybody." Again silence.

"You're a cute son-of-a-bitch, ain't ya. Listen, we're gonna hang onto her for awhile. We've moved things around just so you can make the right decision here. Now, get yourself back to that nice beach house in New Jersey and we'll be in touch again." Rocky wasn't part of the game. I had to get her out.

"You've got the wrong girl. The other one's right here. If she knows anything, I'll . . ." But the line was dead. He had hung up and left me trying to implement plan "B."

Spring break was approaching. Rocky was scheduled to go over to Jacksonville to meet some high school friends. Her parents were spending April and May in Paris. Nobody was going to miss the Tulane co-ed. Except me. Vinny's boys believed they were dealing with an NYU orphan. No next of kin, no worries. They could string it out as long as they wanted. They played the hand they wanted and I had no choice but to go along. They wanted me back in New Jersey. Back on familiar turf, where they wouldn't have to ask for favors they'd have to repay to the New Orleans mob. But if what Deliah had told me was true, Stone Harbor was where I was heading anyway.

-11-

Deliah and I took the streetcar downtown, and from there caught a cab to the airport. I want to at least feel like I was making it difficult for someone to follow us. We flew back to Philadelphia and rented a car to make the familiar drive to Stone Harbor. On the drive, I made Deliah take herself back to that house in Brigantine where she had seen the Columbian being tortured. She tried hard, but there seemed to be certain connections within her brain that didn't quite function. But she gave me as much detail as she could. She even came up with some street names. That was going to be a big help.

The way I figured it, Vinny's boys had taken Adrian and were probably holding her in some safe house. Hopefully they hadn't tried to torture the truth about the Golden Bean out of her. She didn't know the truth. I knew what Deliah had told me, but I wasn't sure if that was the truth either. It was worth the risk to see if maybe the Brigantine house was still being used to hold various hostages and other forcibly invited guests.

We arrived in Stone Harbor around midnight. April had turned into May and the air was finally beginning to warm. Deliah had a key to the beach house. We walked in and I felt like I was returning to the scene of several crimes.

"Is it chilly in here?" Deliah asked. I didn't think it was actually cold, but there was something chilling in the house.

"Yeah, a little," I said. Deliah walked through a door at the back of the first floor and emerged a minute later with an armful of firewood.

"You know how to start a fire, Branach?" she asked snidely.

"I think I could manage." I built a fire in the upstairs fireplace as Deliah rooted though the canned goods left in Liza's pantry.

"There's some chicken-noodle," she said from behind the pantry door.

"Sounds good," I said, and picked up a notepad off of the coffee table by the phone. I wrote everything Deliah had told me about the Brigantine house out on the notepad. We ate the chicken-noodle soup then she went to bed and I stayed there looking over the notepad. In the morning I went down to the Stone Harbor library and got a hold of a map of Brigantine. I sat in the little room at the end of the Borough Hall that housed the town's small collection of books and maps and memorabilia. A Stone Harbor cop walked through, gave me a passing glance, then disappeared into one of the stacks. He reappeared a moment later and gave me a good once-over. I ignored him.

I narrowed the location of the house down to two addresses in Brigantine. I folded the map and returned it to the librarian. She was a quiet lady in her seventies. When I handed her the map I saw a slight flutter of recognition in her eyes.

"Are you?" She paused and lifted her wire-rimmed, round lensed glasses from her desk. Putting them on, she took a step back from me. "You're Thorpe Branach. My goodness, I use to baby-sit you. Mrs. Russ. You might not even remember me." I didn't, but I acted like I did. "I was so sorry to hear about your mother Thorpe, she was a great lady."

"Thanks Mrs. Russ, she always thought fondly of you." As she talked, I looked over my shoulder and noticed the cop was listening to the conversation. "Mrs. Russ, I apologize, but I've got to meet a friend and I'm already late." She was understanding and let me bow out of the conversation.

I hurried out of the library and was almost hit by a car coming out of the drive-thru at the bank next door to the Municipal Building. Back at the house, I called information to try and get phone numbers for the two Brigantine addresses. The operator read me the first number then started hunting for the second. I could hear the keys of her computer keyboard clicking as I held on the line.

"I'm sorry sir, the other number is non-published. I'm afraid I can't give it to you." She said finally. I thanked her and hung up. This was the house I was looking for.

* * *

If you're going to take on professionals you need two things, a plausible diversion and a gun. I learned a trick a few years back about getting metal objects onto airplanes. It takes two people and a less-than-attentive security crew

The day we left New Orleans, I wore a green rain poncho with a large, floppy pocket on the back of it. Deliah followed close behind me, dressed in a tight, white sweater and a black and white checked miniskirt. She turned a few heads. I went through the metal detector first and stumbled just a bit as I came through. Deliah collided with me for a split second, just as the metal detector went off.

"Um, could you please step back through?" The security officer manning the metal detector was a black man of about fifty. He smiled at Deliah and she smiled back as she walked through the metal detector again. I was halfway down the concourse by now. She walked through and set it off again. Then she struggled to unclasp the large metal necklace from around her neck. Finally, she asked the security man to help her, which he gladly did. Without the necklace, she passed through without setting the machine off. By this time I was sitting on a little plastic bench watching the plane that would take me to Philadelphia taxi into the gate. My little .38 was a heavy lump in the bottom of my poncho pocket, right were Deliah had dropped it when we collided.

Now I was in Liza's guest room, cleaning it and loading it with six, hollow-point bullets. Shooting one of Vinny's boys would certainly be the worst-case scenario, but as the cops say, better to be judged by twelve then carried by six. It was a Wednesday morning. The sky was trying its absolute hardest to be blue. But the gray of a long, cold winter was still hanging over the little barrier island, my once and future home. I slipped the gun into my small, black duffel bag and walked out onto the deck. In my mind's eye, I could see Liza once again. I shook my head as if I could rattle the memories out of it. But they persisted. That is until I saw a splash in the surf about thirty yards off the beach. I concentrated on the area and soon saw the bobbing dorsal fins of a score of Atlantic porpoises. They spouted and splashed and occasionally broke free of the water entirely. I let my mind travel with the porpoises. I swam with them and rode the shore-break with them. I was off to the depths of the sea where the Vinny DeScarpas of the world were powerless, helpless creatures.

"Oh my God! I can't handle this." Deliah shouted from inside the house. I turned and looked through the open sliding-glass door to see her ball-up a piece of paper and throw it against the wall.

"Woah!" I said, as I walked off the deck. "What is it?" I picked up the crumpled piece of parchment and flattened it between my palms.

"You are something else Branach. You toss around with a desperate divorcee for a couple of months and ten years later you're moving into her house." I read the letter in disbelief. It was a legal letterhead with the names of about sixty attorney of various bars.

NOTICE TO HEIRS

Be advised that the Last Will and Testament of Liza Debeneaux Grey will be executed by this office in accordance with the laws of the State of New Jersey and the wishes of the testatrix. Said Last Will and Testament contains a general bequest of all the residue of the estate into trust for the benefit of Deliah Debeneaux until her attainment of the age of thirty years and a specific bequest of the property at 100, 132nd Street in Stone Harbor, New Jersey, and all improvements thereto, in fee simple to

Thorpe Branach of 1645 Huey Long Court, New Orleans, Louisiana. Challenges to these bequests must be made, in writing, to this office, no later than December 20.

It finished with a "Most Sincerely" from some guy with a bunch of extra letters after his name. I tried not to smile. Deliah was trying not to explode. I could see the heat in her eyes. She had true contempt for me. But this went beyond her limits. I was taking a part of her mother from her. I was now the owner of the beach house where Deliah had entertained and impressed her tourist friends and college sweethearts.

"Look, Deliah, we can worry about this later. I don't have time to argue about these things now. I've got to get Adrian away from these scumbags before they realize she isn't you and dump her in the pine barrens somewhere." She stiffened at my comments. "We can straighten this all out later. Right now I need you to be a little stable in case I need your help." I didn't expect her to, but she got herself together. She took a deep breath, placed her hand over her eyes and then exhaled all in one big sigh.

"All right," she said as she moved her hand away from her face and looked at me. "I'll do my best." I was flabbergasted at this change of demeanor.

"Thanks," I managed to say. Deliah walked downstairs and left me to my notepad and the sketch of Brigantine I had made from the library map. Now all I needed was a plan.

I took my wallet out of the back, right pocket of my jeans. From it I pulled the small, crumpled bar napkin upon which was written the number of The Cubano's friend in New York. I wanted to call. I wanted to cash in all the old man's chips and get Adrian back without a struggle. But that would expose The Cubano to the possibility of being found by people he had avoided for thirty years. He was an honorable and loyal man who would have gladly traded places with the young, kidnapped girl from Tulane.

I folded the paper up and put it back in my wallet. If I was going to expose my old friend to danger, it was only going to happen after I had exhausted every angle I could handle myself.

THE GOLDEN BEAN

-12-

The sun was setting over the marshlands to the west as I headed north up the Garden State Parkway. I exited the parkway and stopped at a gas station in Smithville. The attendant dropped his cigarette out of his mouth without using his hands and crushed it out with his foot as he reached for the pump. His hair was slicked back but mussed-up in spots. He had a two-day beard speckled with engine grease. The blue, short sleeve shirt he wore was tucked neatly into his jeans which were smeared with the same grease. Over the left breast pocket was a patch with the name "Jimmy" embroidered on it.

"How much ya need?" Jimmy asked, as he pulled the nozzle from the pump.

"Actually, have you got a bathroom?" I asked. He put the nozzle back on the hanger.

"Oh. Sure man. Let me get the key." Jimmy was a product of that vast area in the middle of the State where North and South Jersey meet. Where Princeton, Elizabeth, Trenton, Philadelphia and Atlantic City all try to exert their influence. He probably attended the local community college. Worked as a mechanic and gas jockey. And would end up moving to Florida a week before his thirtieth birthday leaving his wife and three kids behind. He was the inspiration for a kid from Freehold who became The Boss. A few moments later he arrived with the bathroom key.

"Thanks," I said as I took the key from Jimmy and headed for the restroom. Once inside I took the .38 out of the briefcase I was carrying. I dropped the gun into the right, side pocket of the blue blazer I was wearing. I looked in the mirror and strengthened my red tie. It looked sharp against the brilliant-white, cotton oxford shirt. I reached into the pocket of my khakis and pulled out the Zippo lighter I had bought at the airport in Philly. I lit a Punch, Corona-sized cigar, drawing the lighter flame into the tobacco with each puff. Once I had the cigar burning well, I pulled a small bottle of Jim Beam out of the inside pocket of the blazer. I didn't drink any of it. I slapped it on my face like cologne. I swished it around in my mouth and spit it out like mouthwash. I even ran some through my hair.

Finally, I stood and looked at myself in the mirror. Clean-shaven and well dressed I could pass for the young businessman who was married to a bottle and a desk instead of a wife. I had the five-o'clock-shadow and the weathered briefcase. Only I didn't have any market data or accounting figures in the briefcase. I had a pair of bolt-cutters, a bag of plastic zip-strips and roll of silver duct tape, to which I added what was left of the bottle of bourbon.

Jimmy started walking toward me as I exited the bathroom. I tossed him the key and put a little bit extra on the throw. The key went over his right shoulder despite his best effort to catch it.

"Sorry." I shouted as I got in the rental and headed off toward Brigantine. I drew hard on the cigar and blew the smoke out the window. For reassurance I reached into the left side pocket of the blazer and fumbled with the big smoke bomb I had with me. A teenager's prank was the basis of the life-threatening plan I had come up with. I zig-zagged through the streets of Brigantine, a bit paranoid that the nosey Stone Harbor cop had decided to follow me.

* * *

I could taste the adrenalin as I arrived at the house I was looking for. I pulled abruptly and awkwardly into the empty driveway. I moved as quickly as I could toward the front door, a jumble of keys in my right hand. I got to the door just as one of Vinny's boys was approaching from the inside. This was definitely it. I saw two other men in shirt-sleeves standing attentively inside. I fumbled with the keys, lurching and swaying as I had crossed the porch, never lifting my eyes from the lock on the door. I picked out a key and tried to shove it into the deadbolt on the door.

"Eh! Eh! What the hell ya doin'?" I ignored the protests of the man behind the door. He pressed his face toward the little diamond shaped widow in the middle of the top half of the door. "Beat it jerkoff, you got the wrong house." I continued my search for the right key and paid no attention to the shouting man. Finally I heard the deadbolt opening. He cracked the door and shouted through the foot-wide opening, "Pal, you got the wrong housc, go home and sleep it off." I took notice and acted surprised.

"Hey," I said as I leaned against the door. "What da fug are you doin' in my house." I pushed against the door. I saw one of the other men begin to walk toward the door. I wedged myself between the door and the jam and shouted at the pair, swinging my right arm. "You better get the hell outuf my house you bastahs." They opened the door, pulled me in and slammed the door shut. This was the moment. The second in time when everything goes right or terribly wrong. I stumbled and fell and cursed unintelligibly. Unseen, I touched the fuse of the smoke bomb to the lit end of the cigar. I heard it hiss and flipped it toward the middle of the room. It hissed and rolled and smoked wildly. I came up with the brief case and buried it into the side of the head of the man who had first come to the door. I held onto the case with my left hand and pulled the gun from my pocket with my right. Crouching below the thickest smoke, I could see the battered man out cold and bleeding on the floor. I saw a pair of legs bumping into arm chairs and coffee tables. I rushed the legs and brought the second man down. I used the classic, mob-style pistol-whipping to put him out of commission.

The layout of the house was exactly as Deliah had described. I knew it as if I had lived there for years. I hurriedly crawled to the kitchen. The smoke had barely reached there. I crouched in the doorway, beside the wall cabinets. I pushed the briefcase out into the open and heard the rush of a person crossing the room. He was hyped up and rushed the first thing he saw. I emerged and caught him as he was realizing that he was about to attack a briefcase and not a man. The .38 whacked solidly into him, just above the right temple. He was a huge man, older than the other two. He stumbled backwards into the refrigerator and caught himself. I pressed the barrel of the gun into side of his head.

"Turn around, chubby, or I'll paint the wall behind you a nice speckled red." He turned obediently and without being asked, put his hands on top of his head, fingers interlaced. I could just reach the brief case as I crouched and kept the gun on the big man. I took out a zip-strip. The little plastic wonder was designed for binding packages and tightening insulation around pipes. Just a little plastic strip that can only be tightened, not loosened when the flat end is laced through the locking end. They have allowed one cop to secure multiple suspects without a single pair of handcuffs, an unfortunate necessity these days. I zip-stripped his wrists together behind his back.

She was there in the kitchen, handcuffed to an ancient radiator. She was crying and looked like she might pass out.

"I'm so sorry, Rocky. We'll be outta here in a second." She was crying and verged on hysteria. "Hey, hey, got to be strong just for another minute kid. Don't let me down." She actually managed a weak little smile and raised her chin as she took a deep breath. I got the bolt cutters out of the briefcase and snipped the small chain that linked the cuffs. Adrian grabbed me and hugged me with all the strength left in her small frame. "Okay Rock, we've got some things to take care of in a hurry here."

"Okay, Thorpe," she said quitely, as if speaking in a normal voice might awaken some sleeping demon. She helped me duct-tape the hands, feet and mouths of the two men in the living room. One was still out, the other was groggily trying to get to his feet. Then we taped up the big guy in the kitchen. All in all, it was about a four-minute operation.

I drove at a normal pace out of town and back down the

parkway. I hoped that the three men were the night shift and wouldn't be discovered until morning. Stone Harbor, the sleepy little resort town getting more and more active as summer approached, was the perfect place for us to go. You don't get over the 96th Street bridge without being noticed. And if you are not a regular or a local, you are noticed that much more. It wasn't going to be easy for Vinny to just walk into town and take me down.

-13-

Adrian was not in as bad shape as I thought she might be. She had been kidnapped, held against her will and chained to a radiator, but she had not been abused in the way she might have been. That was going to make it one hell of a lot easier for her to overcome the entire ordeal. She showered for over an hour and occasionally I could hear her crying. Deliah gave her a big, terrycloth robe to wear over a pair of flannel pajamas. It was a cold night in early May and the wind was rolling off the Atlantic in frozen sheets. The three of us sat at the kitchen table. Deliah and I answered questions. We didn't ask any. Adrian's confusion slowly lifted and so did the weight of the experience. She fell asleep on the couch, a deep, but restless sleep. Her breathing was heavy and labored. I could see her eyes darting under her eye lids and I imagined that she was having a dream of being chased and maybe even caught by the wolves.

We spent the next month and a half watching Spring arrive and turn into Summer. We walked the beach during the day and slept with all the lights on at night. I installed a cheap but effective alarm system that was occasionally triggered by a rabbit that had hopped out of the bayberrry bushes that blanketed The Point at the south end of the island. We lived comfortably off the estate of the deceased Liza. But no one ever came to even the score. I figured that Vinny must have a few people posing as tourists, maybe even a full-fledged summer rental. But there had been no attempt to even the score, at least not yet.

Actually, it was the right move. Vinny didn't have the Golden Bean. He didn't have the girl. He had nothing but time. Sooner or later, I was going to go after the necklace and he knew that. It was just a matter of keeping a good eye on me and taking me down at the right moment. All the walking and swimming and breakfasts and dinners on the sundeck had made all three of us tanned and relaxed. But the tension was constantly underlying our lives. Sometimes when the phone rang, we'd all jump, startled. An unfamiliar noise in the house at night would have us all huddled in a corner of a room, sleepless until dawn.

* * *

On the morning of June 29th, I called Trent Roberts on his direct line at the Stone Harbor Police Department and asked him if he was missing a badge.

"Branach, you don't make things easy on yourself do you?" Trent said. "You know there are people here who would like to come after you for the death of your old girlfriend. Excuse me, your former, old girlfriend." He snickered into the phone.

"Listen, Trent, I've got a story to tell, but only if you come down here and agree to listen. Otherwise, you stay out in the cold with rest of the putzes working this case." I didn't hear anything for a long second.

"Why'd you take the badge?" he asked finally.

"I'll tell you when you get here," I said and hung up the phone. I was counting on Trent Roberts' sense of destiny to keep him from telling anyone else at the SHPD what he was up to. If Trent could solve the case on his own, he was on his way to being Chief at a very young age.

Trent Roberts showed up in uniform, just as I had hoped. After all, it was summer now, and a Trent Roberts in a white shirt and a shiny badge attracts a lot more attention than one in a tacky sport coat. I just hoped that Vinny or one of his lackeys was watching one of Stone Harbor's finest enter the house.

Trent and I sat on the deck and drank iced tea from tall glasses.

"I hear this is all yours now, Branach. Sounds like motive to me," he said as he squeezed a lemon wedge into his tea.

"Gimme a break, Trent. Innocent men don't respond to idiotic accusations, except to say they're ridiculous, so that's what I say." He squinted at me and nervously ran his fingers over his "scrambled eggs," the gold embroidering decorating the black bill of his hat. "There's one more thing." I said as I placed his detective's badge on the table in front of him. "I only talk if you agree not to ask me why I took the badge." He sat there for a long, thoughtful second.

"All right, all right Thorpe. I'm not gonna bust your stones over any of this, as long as I hear something worth listening to."

I told Trent Roberts a version of recent events that was plausible and would hold up to scrutiny. I wanted to stir up the pot enough to scare Vinny's people out of town and maybe even get some of them locked up. I expanded on the story I had told the lie detector just a couple months earlier. I explained how the man in the pictures with Liza was one Vinny DeScarpa, a young and ambitious mobster from one of the New York families. I told Trent how Vinny had gotten the same extortion package as Liza. But Vinny thought it was Liza pulling the scam and sent some boys to get the photos out of her. Things had gone wrong and Liza had bought the farm. He asked me the appropriate questions and I answered with all the right answers. I knew so much because I had some friends that worked for a company called the CIA who had found things out for me. I gave Trent a phone number to call in Northern Virginia that would put him in contact with a man who would actually confirm my assistance to the CIA if given the proper sequence of passwords. It was actually the number of a bar where I once worked in Alexandria. The manager was a very loyal friend.

I became the proverbial confidential informant that gave the information that allowed New Jersey and New York authorities to execute search warrants on several places in both states. My info was conditioned on anonymity and I promised I'd never be a witness. Trent had to hope he could rattle enough cages to get somebody to spill the beans on the murder.

The timing was perfect. By July first, several of Vinny's boys were in custody and out of Stone Harbor. Vinny, however, was out on bond, ordered not to leave the Borough of Queens.

-14-

In Stone Harbor, on the Fourth of July, a thousand or so people gather at the playing fields at 80th Street and First Avenue to listen to music and wait for the twilight fireworks display. Across the street is the Windrift Hotel with the only outdoor bar on the island. It is a beach bar where barefooters can walk up and get a frozen daiquiri or Planter's punch. The Windrift was one of the many places I had worked as a teenager. One summer I was a bellhop, another summer I was the lifeguard. The beach-block at 80th Street is alive and happy on Independence Day.

I arrived early and set down a blanket and unfolded a couple of beach chairs. I carried a large canvas bag that contained beach towels, sunscreen, a little, green, collapsible-metal army shovel and my snub-nosed .38. If I had gone through the paces correctly, and if what Deliah had told me was true, I was sitting right over the spot where she had buried the Golden Bean.

* * *

After that fateful weekend when Vinny DeScarpa had stolen the ancient necklace of the Ethopian King, Deliah had worked her feminine magic to win back Vinny's heart. She convinced him of her hatred for her mother. He let her back into the inner circle of the two-bit hoods who were free-lancing the sale of the Golden Bean. The New Yorker ad was actually Deliah's idea. The first chance she got she snatched the necklace and headed back to the beach.

In the middle of a cold, winter night, she wore her black

jogging outfit and walked one hundred paces from third base of the softball field, then turned right and walked another hundred to the spot where she buried the necklace in a plastic, ziplock bag.

* * *

The grass had been fertilized and cut a dozen times by Stone Harbor's attentive public works crew by the time I arrived on July Fourth. I compensated for Deliah's smaller stride as we had practiced on the beach for weeks.

The noontime sun was beating down hard and hot. I put some sunscreen on my nose and eased back into my beach chair. I left my mirrored sunglasses on and never closed my eyes. As the afternoon wore by, hundreds of tourists and locals filtered in and took up their positions all around me. By five o'clock, when the music started, there were at least a thousand people dancing and eating and celebrating their freedom. Every so often I took a little scoop of dirt out of the ground next to my chair. By seven-thirty I was down about a foot and a half, just above the level where Deliah said she left the zip-locked bag. A few minutes later, I hit the corner of the bag. Another eight inches toward the beach and I would have been right on top of it. It took me some time to dig around the bag. Some people were starting to notice the strange guy digging a hole in the field.

The first test rockets were fired out over the Atlantic off the 80th Street beach, testing the direction of the evening wind. The fireworks exploded and the crowd cheered. The weird guy with the shovel was no longer important. The show was starting.

The sky darkened as the last flashes of a brilliant sunset sacrificed its beauty for the manmade sky-show of the fireworks. The rockets' red glare illuminated the field as the collective "ooo's" and "ah's" of the crowd went up with each explosion. Halfway through the display, I had the hole filled in, my bag packed up and the chairs folded. I tucked the plastic bag with the Golden Bean into the waistband of my swim trunks and headed through the crowd toward 80th Street. I was driving Liza's black, convertible BMW, which was actually Deliah's by now, although I considered it an improvement on the property. It was a pretentious toy in my mind, but it was cheaper than renting a Mitsubishi.

I had closed the trunk and was walking toward the driver's side door when I felt the cold steel of the barrel of a handgun at the back of my neck.

"You ever see a guy who gets shot through the neck? He flops around like a fish. Or he just lays there trying to move arms and legs that'll never budge an inch. Or, if he's lucky, he just dies." He lowered the gun and poked it into my kidneys. "Come on. We goch ya a room over in the Hotel." He reached in my waistband and snatched the Golden Bean. Then he walked me across the street and down the breezeway to the entrance of the Hotel. I prayed that someone I knew would be there working the front desk. But this was July Fourth, everybody was too busy to notice what was going on. We got on the elevator.

"Two, please." the man said and laughed as he jabbed the gun in my ribs. I reached out and flipped the emergency stop button. We both crashed to the floor, the gun spilling from his hand. I kneed him in the groin as we both rose to our feet. He was a big man, six-three, six-four. He wore a blue, New York Giants tank top teeshirt and a pair of black, cotton shorts. The black pelt of his hairy chest poked out from the oval neckline of the teeshirt. A thick, gold chain hung around his neck. He tumbled over and I grabbed for the gun but he kicked it into the corner of the elevator car. I stomped my foot into his chest and he exhaled loudly and painfully. I flipped the emergency switch back to "on," The car lurched upward and the doors opened almost immediately. I kicked him again and grabbed the little plastic bag out of his hand.

In a few seconds I was making my way up the stairwell, toward the roof. I hoped he would go down and search vainly through the crowd. I got to the door of the roof tower and found it locked. It was a light, wooden door that opened in and was secured only by a knob lock. I kicked it once and it budged only a little. I stopped and listened and I heard footsteps in the stairwell. He was coming up, not going down.

"Here I come, you punk. You think you can mess with my boys, bust up my operation and walk away clean? You got another thing comin' pal." I looked over the railing and felt a wind pass my face, then I heard the shot. It buried itself in the concrete of the hotel ceiling above me.

"Jesus, Vinny," I shouted. "You can't just blow me away up here and expect to get away with it." He was silent below. I kicked the door again and it gave a little more.

"I can," he said finally. He was closer now. "That little

thing you got in the ziplock is my ticket outta here for good. What's one yokel corpse in a hotel stairwell?" I heard him take a few steps.

"This ain't Queens, Vinny. Those kinds of things don't happen here." I kicked again. The door was ready to give. I heard him coming closer.

"Its all over now, punk," Vinny said as he rounded the corner at the top of the stairs and leveled the gun at me. The door gave way and I fell through just as a shot from his nine-millimeter ripped a foot-long chunk out of the metal door jamb. I fell onto the floor and clutched at the boxes of toilet paper and coffee filters that cluttered the tower. It was used for storage. I knew there was a door out onto the roof at the back of the tower. I heard a thud beside me as another bullet burst through a box of toilet paper, sending clouds of ignited tissue into the air.

"Goddammit!" He shouted in anger, apparently mad at himself for having missed me three times.

I leapt toward the door to the roof and laid my shoulder into it. The door flew open and I rolled on my right shoulder onto the tar and gravel of the hotel roof. The finalé was taking place. Red, white and blue rockets exploded, lending an eerie, fluorescent hue to the nighttime. Ear blasting bombs shook the sky. The people below cheered and clapped. I imagined they were cheering for me. That they had watched the entire drama of the stairwell.

A moment later, Vinny DeScarpa emerged from the tower, his nine-millimeter held high.

The stream of water from a one-inch, attack-line fire hose could knock down a good sized steer from about twenty-yards. Vinny DeScarpa took it square in the breast bone from about thirty feet. It knocked him backward like a tumble weed hit by a stiff wind. The gun flew from his hand as the water tore the tank top off his back. The boys of the Stone Harbor Volunteer Fire Department always manned the roof of the Windrift during the fireworks. They stomped out embers that blew back off the water from the spent rockets. They tapped into the hotel's standpipe with their hoses just in case. Today they put out a mob punk who got a little too bold for the yokels of this little beach town.

Vinny lay in the roof tower, soaked from head to toe. A couple of the firemen checked him for vital signs, then turned to those of us out on the roof and gave a "thumbs-up."

The fireworks finalé hit its peak as the sky exploded with light and sound. The crashing of the bombs and the brilliance of the rockets announced the defeat of Vinny DeScarpa and the recovery of the Golden Bean.

-15-

We put Vinny away for the attempted murder of Thorpe Branach, although the murder of Liza Debeneaux was never officially solved.

The New York families put the clamps on the DeScarpa family after they learned just how badly Vinny had screwed up. Adrian and I spent many nights together, talking about evil people and how to forget them. We took long walks on the beach and I tried my best to convince her that, if she tried hard enough, she would one day be able to look at me without thinking about those awful days and nights of captivity. But she had to get away. She returned to New Orleans after the summer and mailed me the contents of my apartment.

Deliah went back to NYU and never said a word about the fact that the house was now mine. And the Golden Bean? Well, it wasn't officially part of Liza's estate. It didn't legally belong to anyone except some Ethiopian King who had been dead for over a thousand years. As that summer moved on, Deliah and Adrian and I would sometimes get the necklace out of the new safe, which was securely in the wall. The girls would try it on. We would sit on the deck and stare at it. The braided, gold chain was about eighteen inches long in all. It was encrusted with small jewels, rubys, emeralds and diamonds.

And then there was the Golden Bean itself. A teardrop-shaped hunk of gold as big as a child's fist, hanging from the center of the chain. It was heavy and smooth and glowed as if it had its own light. We would sit, mesmerized, for hours, just staring at it. It was easy to see how Kings and Queens and Popes and Dictators had fought and died in pursuit of the Golden Bean. Something like that, people would continue to fight and die over. So there it sits in my safe. Safe in Stone Harbor. Liza had kept it there for years. I leave the door unlocked when I go out and even when I sleep at night. That's the luxury of living in the last small town in America.

-16-

The sun was setting as I drove another rental car. This time it was a Suzuki Samurai. I bounced down the mountain road that led to The Cubano's estate on Dominica, the crown jewel of the Caribbean. Stephania stood, leaning against one of the marble columns at the top of the broad stairs that led to the front door, her long, dark hair moving with the warm evening breeze.

"Any room at the Inn?" I asked as I got out of the car. She pulled a powder-blue cardigan tightly around her and walked toward me.

"There may be a spare room where you could stay for the night." She stood, tip-toed, and kissed me on the lips. I took her in my arms and kissed her back. The star-spangled sky looked down on us. Somewhere out in the fading light, a dog was howling. I imagined it was the wolf. He was angry that he had failed once again, but he was still out there. He was howling to let me know he would be waiting.

"I was hoping I could stay for more than just a night," I said to Stephania. She took me by the hand and led me toward the house.

"You can stay as long as you like," she said, smiling. "How was your summer?"